What Reviewers Say A

"With its expected unexpected tw........ .... dose of humor, *Blind Curves* is a very fun read that will keep you guessing." – *Bay Windows*

"In a succinct film style narrative, with scenes that move, a character-driven plot, and crisp dialogue worthy of a screenplay ... the Richfield and Rivers novels are ... an engaging Hollywood mystery ... series." – *Midwest Book Review*

Force of Nature "...is filled with nonstop, fast paced action. Tornadoes, raging fire blazes, heroic and daring rescues... Baldwin does a fine job of describing the fast-paced scenes and inspiring the reader to keep on turning the pages." – *L-word.com Literature*

In the Jude Devine mystery series the "...characters seem fully capable of walking away from the particulars of whodunit and engaging the reader in other aspects of their lives." – *Lambda Book Report*

Mine "...weaves a tale of yearning, love, lust, and conflict resolution ... a believable plot, with strong characters in a charming setting." – *JustAboutWrite*

"While these two women struggle with their issues, there is some very, very hot sex. If you enjoy complex characters and passionate sex scenes, you'll love *Wild Abandon*." – *MegaScene*

"*Course of Action* is a romance ... populated with a host of captivating and amiable characters. The glimpses into the lifestyles of the rich and beautiful people are rather like guilty pleasures ... a most satisfying and entertaining reading experience." – *Midwest Book Review*

The Clinic is "...a spellbinding novel." – *JustAboutWrite*

"*Unexpected Sparks* lived up to its promise and was thoroughly enjoyable ... Dartt did a lovely job at building the relationship between Kate and Nikki." – *Lambda Book Report*

"*Sequestered Hearts* ... is everything a romance should be. It is teeming with longing, heartbreak, and of course, love. As pure romances go, it is one of the best in print today." – *L-word.com Literature*

"*The Exile and the Sorcerer* is a mesmerizing read, a tour-de-force packed with adventure, ordeals, complex twists and turns, and the internal introspection of appealing characters." – *Midwest Book Review*

The Spanish Pearl is "...both science fiction and romance in this adventurous tale ... A most entertaining read, with a sequel already in the works. Hot, hot, hot!" – *Minnesota Literature*

"A deliciously sexy thriller ... *Dark Valentine* is funny, scary, and very realistic. The story is tightly written and keeps the reader gripped to the exciting end." – *JustAbout Write*

"*Punk Like Me* ... is different. It is engaging. It is life-affirming. Frankly, it is genius. This is a rare book in that it has a soul; one that is laid bare for all to see." – *JustAboutWrite*

"*Chance* is not a novel about the music industry; it is about a woman discovering herself as she muddles through all the trappings of fame." – *Midwest Book Review*

Sweet Creek "... is sublimely in tune with the times." – *Q-Syndicate*

"*Forever Found* ... neatly combines hot sex scenes, humor, engaging characters, and an exciting story." – *MegaScene*

Shield of Justice is a "...well-plotted...lovely romance...I couldn't turn the pages fast enough!" – Ann Bannon, author of *The Beebo Brinker Chronicles*

The 100th Generation is "...filled with ancient myths, Egyptian gods and goddesses, legends, and, most wonderfully, it contains the lesbian equivalent of Indiana Jones living and working in modern Egypt." – *Just About Write*

Sword of the Guardian is "...a terrific adventure, coming of age story, a romance, and tale of courtly intrigue, attempted assassination, and gender confusion ... a rollicking fun book and a must-read for those who enjoy courtly light fantasy in a medieval-seeming time." – *Midwest Book Review*

"*Of Drag Kings and the Wheel of Fate*'s lush rush of a romance incorporates reincarnation, a grounded transman and his peppy daughter, and the dark moods of a troubled witch—wonderful homage to Leslie Feinberg's classic gender-bending novel, *Stone Butch Blues*." – *Q-Syndicate*

In *Running with the Wind* "...the discussions of the nature of sex, love, power, and sexuality are insightful and represent a welcome voice from the view of late-20-something characters today." – *Midwest Book Review*

"Rich in character portrayal, *The Devil Inside* is an unusual, unpredictable, and thought-provoking love story that will have the reader questioning the definition of right and wrong long after she finishes the book." – *JustAboutWrite*

Wall of Silence "...is perfectly plotted and has a very real voice and consistently accurate tone, which is not always the case with lesbian mysteries." – *Midwest Book Review*

I DARE YOU

by

Larkin Rose

2008

I DARE YOU

ISBN 10: 1-60282-030-9
ISBN 13: 978-1-60282-030-2

This Trade Paperback Original Is Published By
Bold Strokes Books, Inc.
New York, USA

First Edition: September 2008

Credits
Editor: Jennifer Knight
Production Design: Stacia Seaman
Cover Design By Sheri (graphicartist2020@hotmail.com)

Acknowledgments

To the awesome authors at BSB—you guys ROCK! And to the editors who make the pages perfect, you're priceless!

Visit us at www.boldstrokesbooks.com

Dedication

To Radclyffe—thank you doesn't seem near enough. I'm blessed to be part of your family. Oh, and sorry about that morning coronary. Muah!...it was my pleasure...lol.

To the readers—every word, sentence, paragraph, and page, is just for you!

To my children—thank you for loving me no matter who I am. You are all precious to me and my heart would be empty without a single one of you. You still can't read the books until you're married! *grin*

To January...for your quick cut/cut, snip/snip. I can't thank you enough!

To Barbara Karmazin—the beginning of it all for me. Your critiques and friendship are priceless to me. I hope you always know it.

To India Masters...Biatch! Love ya, mean it! Thank you for the motivation...and the need to change underwear. *wink* You're the best!

To my critique group, Erotic Romance Crit Corner, I love you all and I'm so very proud of each and every one of you.

And finally, to Rose. You're still the one! I love you.

Chapter One

From between the folds of the curtain, Kelsey Billings watched from backstage as the patrons milled into the bar. It was Friday, another night she would waste entertaining drunken women with drool glistening at the corners of their mouths. This job was for the birds. She could get better tips, and better service, from the new gay bar three blocks away. But friendship kept her here. And a need of her own. Not for the money.

She let the curtain close and returned to her dressing room. That is, the tiny closet she was obliged to call a dressing room. She collapsed into the only chair and stared at her reflection.

"I'm too damn old to be dancing anymore." She cupped her B-size breasts through the flimsy silk halter top and lifted them a fraction of an inch. "Even my tits are sagging."

"Are you talking to your tits again?" Darren Taylor breezed into the room and plopped his bony ass on her dressing table. "You're only thirty-one and you have a sweeter ass than any of the chickadees in this godforsaken place." He turned to the mirror, licked his index finger, and rubbed it across his eyebrow. "The women cream their panties when you step on that stage."

"I don't want those women creaming their panties or putting their filthy hands on me."

"Then why the hell are you working here, goofball?"

"Because I love dancing and it takes me away from the real

world. Besides, Sharon needed someone to help bring this place alive again."

Kelsey knew her answer was good enough for her best friend. Darren was one of only a few people who knew about her real life—that of managing a multi-million-dollar corporation, of binding herself inside business suits, hair pinned tight into an elegant French braid she hated.

He slid off the table and pointed in the direction of the stage. "Go out there and help your friend." He puckered his whore-red lips, adjusted his flowing wig, and then strolled out the door.

"Loser," Kelsey mumbled after him.

"I heard that, bitch."

Chuckling, she rolled the eyeliner under her lids one last time and blew a kiss to her reflection. "Go get 'em, tiger."

She stood up and fluffed out her waves to show off the platinum highlights, then pulled on a thin black mask. She didn't dare take a chance on anyone recognizing the other Kelsey, a woman who tore companies apart and inspired admiring feature articles in the business pages. Here, at The Pink Lady, she could let go of her inhibitions. She didn't want to lose that freedom.

Tugging down the tiny leather skirt that barely covered her ass, she headed back to the curtain and took another look through the gap. The room was filled to capacity, every chair occupied and women lining the walls, waiting for the lights to darken and the strippers to begin their seductive routines.

Whistles and cheers erupted as the lights dimmed and DJ Max's raspy voice boomed through the speakers. "Anyone ready for some fine asses?"

Kelsey held her breath and waited for her stage name to echo through the room.

"Introducing our star…Veronicaaaaaa!"

The music blared and she slicked her leg through the curtain, running it seductively up and down the edge. Whistles deafened her as she emerged, rocking her hips and sinking to the floor. She twisted around, then shot her ass out toward the screaming crowd, running her fingers seductively along her black lace stockings while she rose with the rumble of drums. The crowd went wild, screaming obscenities as she strutted to the edge of the stage a few feet above the women, then sank to the floor on her knees. Even a few cross-dressers were squeezed in among the dykes, just as eager to join in the fun.

With fingers spread, she ran her hands over her breasts, along her slim stomach, and between her legs, dipping a single finger across her crotch. A woman reached out. Kelsey grabbed her hand, took a single finger, and licked the tip before running it around her hardened nipple over the thin material of her top.

The woman's mouth sagged open. She stared at Kelsey's breasts as if they were suckers and she needed to get to the center of the Tootsie Roll Pop. Dropping her hand, Kelsey got up and sashayed to the stool in the middle of the stage, rolling her hips provocatively with every step. With her hands on the flat wooden stool top, she spread her legs and slowly bent over. She ran a fingertip between the cheeks of her ass and dragged it forward over her crotch. The beat of the music pounded as she dipped to the floor, shooting her ass out toward the crowd again. When she turned and sat, drawing her knees to her chest, the women in the front row were virtually pawing the stage.

With her weight braced, she lifted her legs in the air and let them fall open. The crowd roared and craned while she displayed her covered crotch. They'd have to use their imaginations if they wanted to know what her pussy looked like. Only a few carefully chosen women had the pleasure of sinking their face between her legs. Call her picky, she didn't care.

She clamped her legs together and pushed away from the stool. A gold painted pole climbed from the stage to the ceiling a few feet behind her. She wrapped a leg around it and hunched her crotch against the cold metal. The pressure sent heat burrowing between her legs, reminding her she was long overdue for a fuck.

She slid down until she reached the floor then crawled like a cat on the prowl across the stage, coming dangerously close to a forest of extended hands.

Her knees neared the edge, close enough for fingers to run along her stockings and garter belt. She allowed a fortunate few to fondle her tight legs while she cupped one breast and slipped the spaghetti strap over her shoulder, revealing tanned skin to the vultures below. She pushed the other strap from her shoulder and covered both breasts as the top fell around her hips. Sometimes a tantalizing peek offered more stimulation than full nudity, so she exposed only tiny glimpses of flesh through her fingers. The drooling gawkers screamed and catcalled, reaching for her, trying in vain to grab hold. She licked her lips, raising an eyebrow and hopefully their blood pressures, as she began to fondle herself, sighing and moaning in a pantomime of sex, right on stage.

"Let me do that for you, baby," yelled a woman with a crew cut and drunken leer.

Kelsey gave her a seductive smile, pushed up her breast, and flicked out her tongue, tracing the length of her nipple. Liquid heat crashed between her thighs, and the cries of excited, lusty women fueled the desire coursing through her veins. She really needed to be fucked tonight. Hard.

She imagined her nipple being sucked while fingers were diving into her. Her pussy throbbed in anticipation. She let her nipple poke from her other hand and gave it equal treatment, teasing the frenetic throng until she felt every gaze plastered on her. With the banging closure of the song, she spread her arms and fell back while whistles shrilled around her. She was still for a moment, reveling in the power she had to reduce them all to moist putty, then she rose to her feet and gave the ogling women a saucy wink before exiting through the curtain and shutting them out.

Waiting backstage for his cue, Darren stamped his red high heel and gave her a playful pout. "I so hate going out there after your fine ass has gotten them all shook up. All the delicious men get pushed to the back. It's just not fair."

Kelsey dragged her mask off. "There's a couple in the front I think might interest you."

Darren peeked out. "Hot damn, Mama is coming!"

He yanked the curtains aside and an immediate tension buzzed through the room. Darren was hot sex personified, his electric routine whipping his audience into a frenzy. Kelsey watched him work them for a few seconds then escaped to her dressing room and plopped into the chair. She was free to mingle with the customers now, but being mauled was not on her mind tonight, unless it was by familiar hands. Finding one of her regular fucks was what she wanted.

Her personal favorites were etched into the erotic black book in her mind. Pam? No, she'd found a steady girlfriend now, thank God...hands off. What about Sharon? Hell, no. Kelsey had stopped sleeping with her the second she took this job. She didn't mix business with pleasure, even though, ultimately, she was mixing pleasure with business. Still...another scratch. Roxy slipped into her mind. Um...hello? She'd moved away, like, three months ago. Shit. Surely, she could come up with a few more contenders. How could that little black book have such slim pickings? Was she that choosy?

Sharon poked her head around the door frame. Her narrow face bore the fine lines of stress. She grinned. "Interested in a lap dance?"

"Are you offering or asking?"

Sharon entered the room, black slacks wrapped tight around her long legs. She bent down and nibbled Kelsey's ear. "Am I going to have to fire you just to fuck you again?"

"As a matter of fact, yes." Kelsey wanted to yank Sharon's face between her legs and ride it until hot come spewed from her, but she pushed the thought away, reminding herself again that she had boundaries, that Sharon was her employer and friend first, and a great fuck second. "Who wants the lap dance?"

"A delicious looking piece of ass, that's who." Sharon straightened herself up in the mirror. "She's waiting for you in the back room."

Kelsey raised her eyebrows. She was the one who made the decisions about who she lap-danced for, and she didn't take many women to the small, quiet room away from the main bar.

"I thought you'd want some privacy," Sharon said with a knowing smile. "I'm jealous already."

❖

The woman had her back to the door. Below that back was a fine ass contoured by a pair of carpenter jeans. Dark, wavy hair kissed the nape of her neck. Her hands were tucked into her pockets, expanding wide shoulder blades. Kelsey had a mental image of riding her like a derby rider, using her hair as reins, screaming with pleasure while she creamed all over her back. She blinked hard, pushing the image out of focus so she could concentrate on her job.

The woman turned slowly, her gaze roaming the walls. The profile of a hard-chiseled jaw and a slightly crooked nose came into view. Her hair was short on top and feathered back at the sides. Tanned arms filled out the short sleeves of her peach golf shirt. A jade-green gaze roamed over Kelsey like hot fudge oozing over the side of an ice cream cone. Heat licked a path straight to her clit, making it throb. Her heart strummed in her ears.

She tightened her legs together, easing the throb searing through her crotch. "Is there something I can help you with?"

The reply came in a deep, steady voice. "I was hoping to get a dance." The eyes dropped to Kelsey's hardened nipples.

"Thirty bucks on the table."

Kelsey closed the door and went over to the stereo. When she glanced back, bills were lying on the table and the woman had sunk into the plush chair. Kelsey flipped to her song of choice.

She'd played it so many times it should be the only one on the CD. Music blared from the speakers. The strobe lights pulsed with rhythm around them. Kelsey walked around the woman's chair, running her fingers up a lean arm and across a broad shoulder, until she stood behind her.

"No touching. I do that." She leaned over and licked the woman's ear, smiling as she watched her eyes flutter shut.

She liked the control she had when she gave lap dances. She could do what she wanted and allow what she wanted. Right now, she wanted to straddle this gorgeous woman's face.

She ran her fingers between the firm breasts to the curves of a six-pack stomach, inching her way toward the loose jeans. She nibbled the woman's neck, raked her nails down a firm arm, then moved in front of her. Raw need was plastered in the depths of the woman's eyes, making Kelsey wetter than she already was. If that were possible.

Hiking her leg on the arm of the chair, she rocked her hips toward the woman's face and inched her fingers over her wet pussy. The woman mouthed something as Kelsey straddled her and dropped into her lap.

"Yes?" Kelsey prompted.

The answer was quietly spoken. "I dare you to kiss me."

Kelsey shook her head and turned herself around in the woman's lap. Scooting her ass all the way back until she encountered that sexy, grooved stomach, she began to grind her hips. Strong fingers slid around her waist before working down between her legs. Kelsey moved them aside and rose to her feet, shaking a finger in a no-no gesture.

The woman rose with her and pulled Kelsey against her hard body. "When you spread your legs, make sure you dry your wet crotch first."

Kelsey's heart hammered in her chest while fire licked her inner thighs. She controlled the impulse to sneak a peek between her legs to see how big her wet spot actually was. Hard green eyes met hers. The woman reached for Kelsey's mask. Kelsey jerked back, but she was held tight by arms stronger than her own.

The woman smiled. "I want to see more than just those gorgeous blue eyes. I want to see who I'm taking home tonight."

Her mouth clamped down on Kelsey's, igniting an inferno. A tongue slithered between her lips. Her insides instinctively coiled with need. Holy shit, she wanted this woman's fingers rammed inside her, twisting and turning and forcing her over the edge. The warm lips slid down to Kelsey's throat.

"Take off your mask," the woman urged, sucking skin between her teeth.

All Kelsey wanted was to yank the hot stranger's head back and bite the shit out of her, then climb over her hips and hunch against her until the fire between her legs burned itself out. As if willed by some great power, she found her hands fumbling for the mask. She lifted the edge, revealing her face to the woman she wanted to ride like a stallion, not knowing why she'd done so.

The woman studied her like she was the most breathtaking creature she'd ever seen in her life. "Are you taken?"

Kelsey's stomach knotted. She felt like a beauty queen standing on a stage instead of a stripper in the backroom giving a lap dance. She shook her head. Or did she? Perhaps an earthquake was vibrating her insides.

"No," she whispered.

"Good." The woman drew back, almost spilling her onto the floor. She helped Kelsey get her balance, then stalked to the door like a tornado whipping through Kansas.

The sex-starved high still ran like hot lead through Kelsey's veins. She wished she were still straddling the firm body, anonymous and following her own rules. She wished she'd just imagined letting her burning need for sex override her common sense. But the eyes staring back at her proved the kiss had taken place. Then came the final taunt.

"I dare you to want more."

She was out the door before Kelsey could call her all the things that echoed through her mind. *Loser, tease, bitable, edible... Hey, get your fucking ass back in here and clean up the mess you made.* She was in awe of the woman's nerve. *I dare you to want more?* Hello? *What fucking grade were they in? Sally, I dare you to kiss Eugene on his pee-pee.* She whirled around and punched the off button, praying this was all just some sick dream and she hadn't revealed her face to a total stranger...a stranger she still wanted between her legs, making her howl with pleasure.

Kelsey stared into the empty hallway. "Who the fuck was that?"

Chapter Two

Jordan Porter eased onto a stool at the bar. Her crotch throbbed for the woman who'd just flopped around in her lap like a rag doll. She'd wanted to fling Veronica—or whatever her real name was—on her back, open her legs like a pocketbook, and feast on her. The moment the luscious blonde had erupted onto the stage, Jordan knew she wanted nothing more than to feel that scrumptious body shake and tremble under her weight, to hear moans rumble from that delicate throat. She couldn't remember feeling such instant, gut-wrenching need spiral inside her for anyone. Not even for Marsha, the raving beauty she couldn't get enough of for the first six months of their relationship, then couldn't get rid of for the next year.

After their breakup, freedom rang in her soul like a church bell and she'd vowed not to lose it again anytime soon. She set her sights on women who were already attached—the safest by far—or had careers to worry about and didn't want bothersome relationships to interfere. Besides, Jordan had her own career to think about, too.

But God, how she wanted Veronica.

Jordan imagined she'd be just as good a lover as she was a dancer. Her glares at the audience told Jordan she got no pleasure from seducing them. Nor had she given them the show they really wanted, her bare-naked pussy slithering on the stage. It pleased

Jordan to know she wasn't taken. Veronica could have her pick of any woman in this slimy bar, and outside of it as well. She'd need only beckon to have any one of them follow her around like a lost puppy. But maybe that was too easy for her.

Jordan wondered what it would take to hear her beg. She hadn't believed in lust at first sight...until now. Out of all the women she'd had the pleasure of making love to, not one had stalled her heart like Veronica. The sight of her sinking to her knees and crawling on the floor like a love goddess made Jordan whine. She was destined to have this woman, meant to make her scream in pleasure.

Without much enthusiasm, she lifted her gaze to the woman dancing on the stage. Fishnet stockings clung to her legs like a second skin. She was pretty, in a schoolgirl kind of way. Her blond ponytail bounced while she danced to the fast-paced song. A red-and-black plaid miniskirt slipped to the floor as she performed her routine. The difference between her and Veronica was stark. Veronica danced to the beat as if she owned it and taunted the audience with all they would never get to touch. The dancer with the ponytail moved as though she'd rehearsed the part just enough to memorize each one-two-three step.

Jordan turned toward the darkened hall once more, and this time Veronica stood at the end with flushed cheeks and pissed smirk, mask back in place over her gorgeous face. Her blond highlights glistened with every passing orb of the strobe light. Jordan's breathing quickened and heat ignited between her legs. She gave a casual nod, not ready to make the next move. How long would it take for Veronica to send a signal?

Her neck tingled as the air behind her stirred and she looked around with the beginnings of a grin. But Veronica passed by without a second look and stopped at a table where a group of women immediately started grabbing at her. A tall woman with a dark crew cut pulled her down into her lap. Veronica threw her arms around the woman's neck, playing her goddess role to perfection. She cast a smug look over the woman's shoulder at Jordan, awakening a green-eyed monster that growled, *"Mine."*

Jordan wanted to bang her head repeatedly on the wooden counter until there was nothing left but common sense. What the hell was she thinking? She'd teased this fine piece of ass, and now another woman would get to take her home and put out the fire. *What now, moron?* She dared another glance in Veronica's direction. Their eyes met. Jordan flashed an aroused smile, feeling the need to jump off the stool and drag her to a secluded part of the bar.

The crew cut woman ran her hand along Veronica's thigh, inching too close to her crotch for Jordan's liking—as if she had a right to care one way or the other. Veronica cared, however. She picked up the roaming hand and twisted it, whipping around to face the woman. Something was said, then she threw her long, blond curls around her shoulders, shoved off the woman's lap, and disappeared through a side door by the stage. Red blotches splashed the woman's face.

A trickle of satisfaction crept into Jordan's heart. *I feel your pain, baby. Guess you went too far.* She wondered how far Veronica would let *her* go? Something told her she'd get exactly what she wanted if she played her cards right. Determined to find out, she eased off the stool with heat traveling between her legs and a hard fuck on her mind.

❖

"Goddamn women!" Kelsey shoved cash from the lap dance into Darren's tip jar and slammed into her dressing room. She ripped off the mask and tank top and grabbed her bra from the chair.

"Who you screaming at now?" Darren asked from the doorway.

"Everyone." Kelsey continued changing her clothes,

swapping the miniskirt for a pair of low-slung jeans. "They think I'm rare meat on a plate."

"Honey, the way you crawl around that stage hiding all the goodies, you can't expect anything less." Darren strolled into the room, completely free of stage makeup. "They all want to see what they're missing out on."

"Duh. If I wanted them to *see* the goodies, I'd show them." Kelsey slunk to her chair. "I'm so tired of the cheap shit that comes in here."

Darren plopped onto her couch and pointed out the obvious. "Well, you don't have to dance. It's not like you need the income."

"You know why I do it." She met his quizzical eyes. "*Sharon* needs the income, and you and I can sure pull in a crowd."

He sighed. "As much as I hate to say this, you've never fit in here. You're smart and gorgeous, and have a body to die for. Most of the women out there are only looking for a one-nighter, not that they could keep up."

"Tell me about it." Kelsey pulled her hair into a clip. "Let's get the hell out of here. A movie, dinner, doing each other's hair…I don't care."

He gave her his schoolboy smile. "Can't. One of those hunky men invited me to his house for some hot sex."

"You dog. I'm so jealous." She slipped on her belly shirt. "Let me guess. Tall, brown hair, pretty smile?"

"How could you tell?" Darren snickered.

"He sure wasn't waiting for *me* at the edge of that stage." She giggled. "Play safe, you sex maniac."

"Always do." He turned to leave, then jumped back, his hand covering his heart dramatically. "Ooh, honey. You scared the shit out of me."

A woman stepped inside the door frame. Kelsey's heart jammed as she wondered how she'd managed to slip past the bouncer.

Darren moved around her, mouthing to Kelsey, "Do this. Do this."

He ducked away, leaving her alone with the tease from the back room. Her crotch soaked instantly.

"What could you possibly want?" Kelsey asked.

"To see if you're free for the night."

"Why?" Liquid heat licked its fiery tongue between Kelsey's thighs. She longed to squeeze her legs together to ease the ache but wouldn't dream of letting this woman see her squirm.

"Why not? Or did you have some 'cheap shit' in mind?"

Kelsey gave her a sarcastic smile. "Well, at least the cheap shit would finish what they started, if I gave them the chance."

Tension spiraled inside her. She should've cussed this woman out and sent her on her way instead of admitting she had indeed started something. Why let a stranger know she had the power to arouse her?

Raw determination glimmered in the gorgeous green eyes. "Oh, I plan to finish what I started."

Kelsey shrugged. "Sorry. I have a list a mile long of people itching to put out this fire. Your help won't be needed."

"What…I don't measure up to the pond life in this place?"

"*You're* in this place."

"So are you. Does that make us even?"

Kelsey gave her a scornful look. "Not really. You came for the free pussy shots. I don't give them."

The woman chuckled. It was hard to avoid her penetrating stare. "Are you ready to get out of here yet?"

Kelsey scrutinized the firm contours of her face. She was even better looking when her smile seemed genuine. Excitement pulsed through her. She could sense the same fierce urgency in the woman she'd chosen.

"I'm game for a fuck. But you leave come morning light."

"Lead the way." The husky invitation was offered with a knowing grin.

Kelsey's mind wandered in a thousand directions as she hurried out to the parking lot. Having this woman finish what she'd started was her prime objective. She wanted rough hands and hardened fingers plunging an orgasm from her body. She stopped in front of her Ford Explorer and invited, "Follow me."

"With pleasure." Her "date" sauntered across the gravel to a Dodge Viper.

Watching the slow, sexy stroll, Kelsey couldn't remember being this excited to be going home with a woman.

❖

Jordan was impressed when a wrought iron gate slid open and the Ford Explorer turned into the pebbled circular driveway of a pale yellow cottage-style house with a red terracotta tile roof. The thirty-minute drive had taken them through some of the most upscale streets in the city. She'd memorized every street name en route so she could find her way back to this beauty.

The strip joint wasn't the kind of place to pay heavily, so she hadn't expected to arrive at a lavish home in a neighborhood like this one. Her thoughts returned to the conversation she'd overheard as she waited outside the dressing room. The slinky cross-dresser had made a comment about "Veronica" not needing the income from her dancing. Jordan wondered what else she did to pay for her secluded, protected life.

She swallowed the lump in her throat and managed to turn off the engine and climb out of the Viper without dropping the keys. Heat traveled down her spine and settled between her legs as she watched the lovely ass in front of her. All she wanted to do was shove this woman through the door and ram her against a wall. She wanted to push her tongue down her throat, bury her fingers inside her, and make her scream over and over.

Stilling the impulse, she crossed the porch and entered a dark hallway. The lock engaged behind her and light splashed the room as she heard a switch flick.

"Would you like something to drink?" Kelsey offered, controlling the urge to yank that peach shirt up and bite at the nipples beneath it.

"No." Raw determination stared back at her. "After sweating for a few hours, we might need water."

Woo, doggy. Make me sweat. Kelsey smiled. That was all it took. The woman closed the gap between them and clamped her mouth over Kelsey's while pressing her flat against the door. Her tongue slid deep, dancing and exploring, drawing a moan from Kelsey. Liquid lava poured between her thighs. She drove her fingers up through the short, silken hair. Groans rumbled inside her chest as she was pressed harder against the wall. Hands tugged at the clasp of her jeans, then gave them a hard yank and dragged them down her legs. Her skin prickled as her bare ass was exposed, then caressed. Kelsey couldn't remember ever wanting someone to fuck her so bad, or so hard.

They sank down together onto the plush carpet. Firm, probing fingers slipped between Kelsey's thighs, caressing her crotch, weaving through her wiry hair. She let her legs fall open, hunching her hips in the air, wanting to feel fingers drill inside her.

"You taste like sweat." The woman sucked at the skin on Kelsey's neck. "Tangy and sweet."

Kelsey wanted to tell her to shut her fucking mouth. The sooner she was taken over that erotic edge, the better. A fingertip passed over her clit. She dug her head into the carpet, arching her chest in the air, prepared to shove this woman's fingers inside her if she had to. She was running out of patience. Her clit pounded with need as the teasing fingertip passed back and forth, sinking slightly inside, then starting the process all over.

"Before I take your fingers and ram them inside me myself," Kelsey gasped out, "what the hell is your name?"

Teeth nipped the skin on her collarbone. "Jordan Porter."

"Well, Jordan, if you don't get on with this, I might be forced to finish without you."

"What's the rush, my sweet thing?" The fingers withdrew from between Kelsey's legs and Jordan rolled on top of her. She grabbed Kelsey's wrists and pulled them over her head, locking them against the floor. With her knees, she pushed Kelsey's legs apart. Her pelvic bone rocked against Kelsey's crotch. "And who do I have the pleasure of making love to tonight?"

Burning heat smoldered between Kelsey's thighs. The fire was almost too much to bear. With a slight hesitation, and no clue why she wasn't afraid to tell this woman her real name, she whispered, "Kelsey."

"Kelsey." Jordan said her name like it was fragile. "I like that name. It's seductive, enticing, and sweet on my tongue... literally."

Kelsey was completely out of patience. Was this woman nothing but a tease? Was she going to torture her with her seductive words and roaming fingers all damn night? With a sexy grin, she sucked Kelsey's lower lip into her mouth, rolling her tongue across it. Kelsey let loose the moan trapped in her throat. Lightning bolts shot across her mind as her eyelids fluttered shut. Hot breath floated across her cheeks, across her parted lips, into her mouth.

"Stop teasing me," Kelsey murmured.

"It only gets better."

Kelsey could believe that. She blinked up into those gorgeous green eyes.

"Relax," Jordan said. "Why rush it?"

"I don't have patience." Kelsey's chest heaved. "Not right now, anyway."

"All good things come in time."

"I'm going to burn alive if you don't hurry." She hated the words spilling from her lips. She was weak, and this woman knew it.

"Well, why didn't you say so?"

She was barely aware of her wrists being freed, of a face

sinking between her legs. The fire burned her alive from the inside out.

Jordan wanted to watch Kelsey writhe a while longer, but her anguished gaze and urgent panting pushed her forward. Nudging her thighs further apart, she spread her pussy lips with her fingertips and ran the tip of her tongue over her clit. Kelsey arched. Her fingernails dragged through the plush carpet. The sound traveled to Jordan's crotch. She squeezed her legs together to ease the throb. She wanted to eat this woman whole, swallow her down, then fall asleep, full and satisfied. She'd never wanted a woman as bad as she wanted this one. She smiled. She had all night to make love to this siren.

Kelsey's moans echoed through the room and she pumped her hips faster, wild with need. Jordan's heart wrenched. She inserted her fingers into the wet depths, stretching her. After several deep strokes, she nursed Kelsey's clit, increasing her pressure. To her amazement, Kelsey froze, her chest high in the air. Jordan felt her fingers gripped while Kelsey screamed. Her hair was yanked as Kelsey grabbed a handful like a set of reins, digging Jordan's face into her crotch.

With her free hand, Jordan moved one of the legs pinning her head like a vise, creating breathing room. She'd never heard such satisfying cries. Her pride swelled while Kelsey yanked the hell out of her hair. After what felt like hours, the grip loosened and Kelsey's arms fell limp.

Jordan eased her fingers out slowly and slithered up her sweaty body. A tingling sensation scraped across her scalp as though her hair follicles were trying to re-root themselves.

"I'd say that was some pent-up energy." She kissed Kelsey's tangy neck.

"Take off your clothes." Kelsey rolled her over, surprising Jordan with her sudden energy. She straddled Jordan's hips. "I'm not done."

❖

Kelsey had never felt so satisfied, but she was far from finished with this woman's skilled hands and luscious body. The pleasure had awakened an insatiable need. Her body was spent of its sexual frustration, but the faintest touch of Jordan's lips on her damp skin brought her to life. She tugged Jordan's shirt away and discarded it. The soft blue glow of moonlight through the slats of her mini-blinds highlighted Jordan's white sports bra. Kelsey dipped a fingertip in her cleavage. A soft moan rewarded the gentle caress. Jordan's lips clamped down over hers. Her tongue dove deep, mating and tasting. Kelsey's nerve endings hummed. Her clit clenched between her legs, and she pumped into Jordan's lean stomach.

"Fuck me again."

Jordan's lips pressed against her neck. "I didn't *fuck* you the first time."

Warmth spread over Kelsey like melted butter. "It's not too late."

"Are you begging?"

Something in Jordan's teasing grin drove Kelsey wild. An inner voice commanded, *Flip her over. Smack that tight ass.* Unable to resist, she eased Jordan onto her back, tore the clasp loose on her carpenter jeans, and yanked them down those lickable thighs. Jordan quickly got rid of her bra and briefs. Shadows played across the ivory flesh of her chest. The tantalizing sight made Kelsey catch her breath. She bent and sucked an erect nipple between her lips, drawing another moan from Jordan. She trailed her fingers down Jordan's six-pack stomach, letting them linger over the sexy ridges. Jordan tensed as she continued her exploration, finally sliding her fingers through the dark fur at the parting of her thighs.

"You like this, hmn?" She teased Jordan's clit and then dove to the hilt inside her.

"A little," Jordan panted in her ear.

Heat spiraled through Kelsey with every moan. Her crotch throbbed to be touched again. She stroked her fingers in and out, reveling in the wetness, until Jordan's hips rose with new urgency. Kelsey slipped her fingers from inside and moved a tip over her clit, circling lightly. She rubbed until Jordan's soft cries penetrated the air, then lowered her face to the wet curls. Pushing Jordan's legs apart, she spread the swollen folds.

Jordan's breath caught. She arched toward Kelsey's mouth.

"In a hurry?" Kelsey teased. Having been left in a back room aching with need, the least she could do was offer payback.

"Are we going to play the tease game?"

"I'm a fast learner." She gave Jordan's clit a lick. "Now it's your turn."

Jordan inched her hips closer for more. "I guess I'm in trouble."

Kelsey dipped her finger inside, added another, then inserted them farther. She could feel the tension coiling inside. She savored a sense of power as Jordan moaned and clenched her hands into fists. She wanted to tease her more, to drag this out, yet those quivering thighs changed her mind. She needed to see Jordan give in completely. She sucked her clit in a steady, constant rhythm until her body constricted and hard, driving pumps gripped Kelsey's fingers. As Jordan's sharp cries flooded the room, Kelsey relaxed her hold and angled her head so she could watch.

Jordan's face was pink and taut with ecstasy. Her body shook and she reached out, obviously needing to be held. Kelsey withdrew carefully and crawled up to collapse beside her. Sweat clung to their bodies. They draped their arms around each other. Jordan kissed Kelsey's forehead, then nuzzled into her.

Well, this was odd, Kelsey thought. She wasn't used to cuddling after sex. What to do? Lie where she was indefinitely, or remind Jordan that they weren't girlfriends and she didn't live here? Warm breaths floated across her chest and she decided to delay for a few minutes. Maybe Jordan gave foot massages or cooked. Now, that would be awesome.

After some time lying in Jordan's arms exchanging caresses,

Kelsey detached herself and reached for her clothes. She rose and snapped on the light switch.

"Thanks for the warning." Jordan blinked against the harsh yellow light. She watched Kelsey dress. "Are you always this... nice?"

"Shoot, no. I get better. I'm the queen of nice. My friends think I'm made of sugar, I'm so damn sweet." Kelsey offered her hand.

Instead of getting up, Jordan stared as if her hand were a snake ready to strike. Then she grasped it and yanked Kelsey down on top of her.

"I thought you said you weren't done?" Jordan began nibbling her ear.

Kelsey smiled. "There's only so much sweating a girl can do in one night."

She avoided a kiss and got to her feet again, this time walking away from the naked body sprawled on her floor. Determined to stick to her play rules, she headed into the kitchen and pulled two bottles of water from her stainless steel fridge. She took a long drink from one, and when she turned around, Jordan was leaning against the food bar, fully dressed. The ice-cold fluid had cooled Kelsey's throat down a notch. Unfortunately it did nothing for the heat that smoldered between her thighs at the sight of Jordan's broad shoulders and tousled hair. She slid a bottle across the counter.

Ignoring it, Jordan eased around the bar and stood between Kelsey's parted legs. She lifted them around her waist. "I'm not ready to end our date."

Kelsey almost choked. "A *date*...is that what you want to call it?"

Jordan eyed her with a curious expression. "Why not?"

"Do I look like I'm into *dating*?"

"I don't know what you're into." Jordan glanced around the black and white kitchen. "But it looks like you do pretty well for yourself. Most strippers don't live like this."

Kelsey raised her eyebrows. "How many strippers do you know?"

A smile deepened the corners of Jordan's mouth. "Was that jealousy oozing from those pretty little lips?"

"Uh…no. There's not a jealous bone in my body. So, where are you taking me to eat?" Kelsey smiled sweetly.

Jordan's gaze roamed her face, then dropped to her crotch. "I don't have to take you anywhere to eat. You, on this stool, will work just fine."

The smoldering embers sparked to life and erupted into fire between Kelsey's thighs. She reached for Jordan once more.

Chapter Three

Jordan awoke with Kelsey's toned arms and sexy legs sprawled across her. She glanced around the bright bedroom. A large entertainment center stood against the wall at the foot of the bed. Double doors screened the contents inside. What was up with this huge, gorgeous house? No stripper she'd ever heard of made enough money to pay for a lifestyle like this. Was Kelsey an escort? A hooker?

Jordan couldn't believe the woman that hid all the yummy from her fans would give it away for money. But something was paying for this house…or someone. She envisioned a sugar daddy, complete with cane and fat bank account. No. That wasn't it. Maybe a rich dyke wanted to have Kelsey's luscious body waiting for her whenever she decided to fly home. Did she jet in from Paris and have her way with her, waltz her around like arm candy for all of Los Angeles to see?

Whoever paid for this house was making a ton of money or giving up an awful lot to provide Kelsey with such surroundings. It was odd that Kelsey would continue stripping under the circumstances. Jordan studied the beauty lying beside her, the one she'd fucked over and over last night. Kelsey was fast asleep with lips parted. Jordan felt the urge to stick her fingertip inside that mouth, to feel her suck it. *Come on, now. The last time you woke up with a woman, it took you a year to get rid of her.*

Kelsey shifted and stretched. She opened her eyes and stared at Jordan, then rolled over to see the clock. "Holy shit. You have to go. I'm late."

"Late for what?" Jordan watched her fine ass flee around the bed and into the bathroom. "It's Saturday."

The hiss of water started. Puzzled, Jordan eased out of bed and followed Kelsey into the shower. Foam slid down her tan body, catching in her bush.

Kelsey flashed her a smile. "Don't start," she said, leaning under the spray of water.

Jordan stepped into her, kissing the outstretched neck, getting a taste of fruity shampoo. She reached around to cup her ass.

Kelsey swatted at her hands. "I'm not kidding. I'm late."

"Surely you can spare a few minutes." She wasn't ready to leave this woman. A few more nights of fucking wouldn't harm anything.

Suds ran over her hardened nipples. Jordan couldn't resist licking the tips.

Kelsey's fingers tangled in her hair. "Okay, maybe a few minutes."

❖

An hour later, Kelsey drove along L.A.'s bustling streets. Her body was still numb from her early morning orgasm, and thoughts of Jordan kept slithering across her mind. She couldn't remember visions lasting this long after sex, normally. Shaking Jordan's face from her thoughts, she tried to concentrate on the tasks waiting for her. Billings Industries was about to take over another pharmaceuticals company and improve its profitability by selling assets and shrinking the workforce. Like many of the smaller companies bought by Billings Industries, this one was living in the past, having its products manufactured in the U.S. instead of China and using local staff for activities that should have been outsourced to India. And they wondered why they weren't competitive.

Bored by the whole idea of the legal takeover process and unhappy to be the villain in another company restructuring, she pulled into the parking lot behind a white brick building. Her father would roll over in his grave if he knew how uninterested she was and that she wanted to give up everything he'd worked for. He would hate her for what she was tempted to do. Why did she have to be the smart one of the family? Why couldn't he have left her brother Kevin in charge?

Kelsey rolled her eyes at the thought. Kevin was a loser. Their father had left him a trust fund instead of giving him responsibilities he would never handle. Kevin lived in Hollywood and pretended to be an actor. He'd recently put money into a movie with himself as the star. It never had a theater release, but went straight to DVD. That didn't stop him from dropping the names of big stars like they were his personal friends. At the moment he was overseas at a film festival, trying to talk himself into a co-producer role on a movie people might pay to see.

Kelsey was relieved. At least when he was out of town she didn't have to worry about the next bombshell. Kevin only spoke to her when he wanted something. She was the one who hired lawyers to get his ass out of trouble, something her dad had done ever since Kevin was a kid. She was the one who put him in rehab and made sure the woman who'd had his baby received child support when Kevin "forgot" to send the checks.

Her brother never bothered to thank her. They'd been close when they were kids. Kelsey wasn't sure when everything changed, but she felt like she didn't know him anymore, and that hurt. With a sigh, she plucked her briefcase from behind the driver's seat, locked the car, and made her way across the asphalt into the gleaming rear lobby.

Her heels clicked on the marble floor as she passed through the elaborate security scan and headed for a pair of heavy glass doors. She'd made this short walk almost every day of her life for the past ten years, starting while she was still in college. Kevin had always taunted her for being a "Daddy's girl" because she was the one chosen to learn the ropes. He resented her, but not because he wanted the top job. He just wanted the prestige that went with it.

The sounds of her strides in the empty hall made Kelsey want to run away. She hated her job in the bar in many ways, but in the security of The Pink Lady she could be herself, or at least partly herself.

Douglas Whitaker rose from his chair as she entered the small conference room. Only a little older than her, he was the one person she was close to in this dull, agonizing place and was almost like a brother. They'd had plenty of years to become close, growing up across the street from each other. They'd remained allies in the business. When her father died two years ago, she promoted Douglas to vice-president in charge of the company finances, a decision that had pissed off several older associates who thought they were owed the job. Douglas knew how she felt about ripping people's lives apart. Over the past few months they'd been working on a plan to change the direction of her father's company.

She dropped her jacket over a chair and poured herself a cup of coffee. As she sat down, she asked, "Got a girlfriend yet?"

Douglas's life consisted of nothing but work, and Kelsey often teased him about needing a nice roll in the hay. He thought *she* needed to settle down.

"Some of us have more important priorities than getting laid," he said.

Laughing, Kelsey removed a few files from her briefcase. "I don't know," she said, opening the planning document. "I don't see how this idea can work."

"Have you given any more thought to just changing the name?"

"What good would that do? If I can't change the company, what good is a name change?"

Douglas leaned back, scowling at her. "What's up with you? Why are you so damn scared lately?"

"I'm not scared."

Kelsey looked away. He'd pegged her for sure. She was scared shitless to change something her father cared so much about, whether she agreed with the way they did business or not. She'd loved her father more than she loved the very breath in her lungs, and she felt guilty over her disdain for his company. Instead of feeling proud, she was ashamed of the lie she was forced to live. His only wish had been for her to assume his role and keep his legacy alive. If she changed the company, she would be ignoring his dying wishes, something that might haunt her for the rest of her life.

The dilemma kept her up at night. To achieve her own desire, she would have to go against the course set by her father. It would be a slap in the face if she failed. She would then have to continue with something that was tearing her heart apart, draining her soul, one takeover at a time.

"I'm damned if I do and damned if I don't." She cut her gaze back to Douglas. "Don't you understand that?"

He covered her hand with his. Sympathy washed over his hard, chiseled face. "Honey, you know your father loved you more than anything in this world. He left you this company because he knew you could handle it. He wouldn't want you to be miserable. Neither would my parents."

Tears stung Kelsey's eyes. Artie and Ellie Whitaker were her father's closest friends and had become surrogate parents to her when he died. Ellie had also filled the void left after Kelsey's mother skipped town. She did the things a mother normally did as Kelsey matured and was always there when she needed someone to confide in. Artie was more reserved than his warmhearted wife, and even at thirty-one, Kelsey still cowered like a child when he scolded her. Douglas was right. They would want what was best for her, but she couldn't fail her father, no matter what. Keeping things the way they were kept her safe from hurting him. He was the love of her life. No one had ever understood her the way he had. He knew her hopes and dreams, shared in every single one of them.

She shook her head and willed her tears to stay put. "I'm not ready to change things."

Douglas removed his hand and folded his arms across his chest. "So you're going to continue to hide for the rest of your life, constantly looking over your shoulder for someone who might put a bullet through your head. Do you think you can find your freedom in that filthy bar?"

"It's my life." Anger took root. Kelsey shoved away from the table. "You know what? Maybe I should just sell the fucking place."

Before Douglas could answer, she stomped off, marching out of the building without looking back. She flopped into her Explorer, hit the ignition, and eased the car into traffic.

"Did I just decide to sell the business without discussing it with myself first?" she mumbled to herself as she waited at a set of traffic lights.

Why not? What was stopping her? Maybe she could move to Hawaii and live happily ever after. She nodded to her reflection, seriously considering the decision that had popped out of her mouth in anger. She only wished she'd done it earlier, instead of waiting until her list of enemies stretched from here to China. There were several people, possibly hundreds, who would love to kick a chair out from under her and watch a noose choke the life from her.

Billings Industries had made her a multimillionaire, so what did she have to lose by selling? She could make sure the company slid into the right hands, hands that would put her new plan into motion. That was of the utmost importance, no matter how bad she wanted out.

❖

Jordan let her last two pupils out and locked the door of the karate shop she was proud to call her own. She waited for the ten-year-olds to get into their parents' cars, then strolled around the back of the building to her Viper. As she settled into her seat she pondered whether to go to The Pink Lady or hit another strip joint along the boulevard. If she went back again so soon, she'd look desperate. But if she didn't go, it would appear as if she didn't want to see Kelsey again, and nothing could be further from the truth. She'd thought all day about sinking between those lean thighs.

Her cell phone buzzed as she reversed out of her parking space.

"Hi, honey." Her mother's voice put a damper on the hot fantasies.

Jordan grimaced, hating that she'd answered the phone. "Hi, Mom."

"Why don't you ever call? Are you working too hard? You know, your body can only handle so much."

"I'm fine, Mom. I compete next month. I have to be ready."

"Bull. You've been beating the shit out of boys since you could walk."

"That's not the same. Besides, this might be my last fight. I'd like to go out with a bang."

"Lordy, that's music to my ears. You could break an arm. Or even worse, someone could snap your neck like a twig."

"Mom, stop worrying so much. I'm thirty-two and it hasn't happened yet."

"I'm a mother. It's my job."

"Speaking of jobs, any bites on the applications you filled out?"

A long sigh greeted her. Her mom hated talking about her inability to find a job, but Jordan couldn't ignore the subject. Her mother wasn't supposed to be living off welfare, in the projects, for God's sake. Yet she wouldn't take Jordan's help, no matter how many times Jordan begged. She managed to sneak food into the house by insisting she was only stocking the refrigerator with things she wanted to eat when she visited. But Lord forbid she pay another bill behind her mother's back. Susan Porter practically took the roof off the tiny apartment when Jordan tried to pay the rent.

"I'm not going to talk about this," she said. "I have food on my table, and electricity to cook it. That's all you need to worry about."

Jordan rolled her eyes and let out an aggravated sigh. "Fine, but I don't know why you refuse to come stay with me. You can't possibly like living around this filth, with drug dealers roaming your building every night. It's just not right."

"Don't worry your pretty little head about that. I'm a tough broad. In my day, I could go rounds with the best of them. Where do you think you got your tomboyish behavior from?"

Jordan didn't doubt for a second that her mother had left her mark, but she wasn't that tough kid anymore. Times had changed. Jordan felt sick that she ran a successful business and drove the car of her dreams but wasn't allowed to help the person she loved most in the world. She didn't understand her mother's stubbornness. Everyone was entitled to their pride, but she sometimes felt her mother was punishing her. If she wanted Jordan to feel guilty and helpless, it was working.

"I love you, Mom," she said, trying to hide her frustration. "I'll call again in a few days."

As the phone clicked into silence, her mind was made up. She'd go to the club and drink away the sound of her mother's voice and the fact that she was living in poverty. A late entrance would imply that she wasn't completely desperate to see Kelsey again, even though she couldn't wait to see that curvy body and pull Kelsey into her arms for another heated kiss.

That is, if Kelsey was willing to turn their one-night fuck into a double.

❖

Kelsey parked the car in the back of The Pink Lady, then pushed her way in.

Darren poked his head around his dressing room and let out a piercing whistle. "You make my dick hard every time you come here dressed in your corporate drag."

"Shut up, pervert."

"Oh, someone's a sourpuss. Come here and give Daddy a wet, sloppy kiss."

Darren ran at her with fingers wiggling and his tongue hanging out in a perfect imitation of Gene Simmons. She squealed and ran into her dressing room. He was hot on her heels as she jumped in her chair and curled into a ball. He wrapped his arms around her, humping her like some horny dog.

"Come on, baby." He made a slurping sound while she squealed and slapped at her ear. "My beautiful, luscious drag queen."

"Get off me, you mutt."

He giggled and backed up. "You're here early. What's up?"

She straightened her clothes. "I wasn't in the mood for real work after my meeting with Douglas."

"Ooh-la-la. Fine piece of ass."

"He's straight."

"Who cares?"

"I'm selling," she said before she could change her mind.

"Well, it's about damn time." Darren plopped down in her lap. "Can I retire to some lavish island with you? Please, Mommy? I'll be a really good boy and do all my laundry. I'll even keep my boy toys in my bed for nightly use." He stuck his thumb in his mouth and wiggled his eyebrows.

"Get off me, you weirdo." She pushed him out of her lap and started unbuttoning her shirt.

"Speaking of weirdos, you got a strange phone call today. Something about killing you. She was talking with one of those voice-changing thingies. I told her you were a black belt and could snap her neck like a twig with your bare hands. She didn't seem too impressed."

He unwrapped a piece of gum and popped it in his mouth as if his words were the most normal conversation in the world.

"Killing me?"

"Yep. Probably some twat you turned down." He smiled wryly. "Don't act like you haven't heard it all before, honey. I was here the night your ex brought that little fireball in."

"True."

An image of Pam's new girlfriend came to mind. Boy, had she ever been jealous of Kelsey. Pam had brought her here one time, a huge mistake. She was completely disrespectful to her little fling and Kelsey decided to show the new girlfriend what a piece of shit she was getting. She'd slithered her sweaty body all over the stage to keep Pam's attention glued to her, and the plan worked for a while. But instead of badgering Pam with jealous words or stomping out of the bar, the girlfriend flipped her attention to Kelsey. She jumped up to the edge of the stage, screaming like a demented fool and threatening to do everything to Kelsey except her hair and makeup.

Poor Pam. She'd never be able to go in another gay strip joint for as long as she bedded that cute little thing. Not that Kelsey gave a shit who Pam dated. She actually felt sorry for the girlfriend, knowing what a flirt Pam could be. Smiling, she removed her bra and chose a halter top from the closet. The call was probably some prank meant to frighten her. Thankfully, she didn't scare easily.

Someone rapped on her door and Darren let out a blood-curdling, high-pitched scream. Kelsey whipped around, heart jamming in her throat. Sharon stood in the doorway, blinking in shock, her hand covering her heart.

"What are you screaming at, you idiot?" She glared at Darren.

"You are seriously *not* going to leave your hair like that, are you?" He fanned his face. "It's against beauty ethics. The fashion gods will weep in misery. Rivers of salty tears will spill through the streets, polluting the reservoirs. Millions will have to be spent on desalination plants. The city will go broke. You have to do something about that head."

Kelsey doubled over with laughter. It wasn't the end of the world after all. Sharon had her hair in curlers.

"You shit." Sharon planted her hands on her hips and gave him a caustic glare. "Take yourself and your wimpy fashion gods the hell out of here."

"Well, excuse me, Cruella de Vil. With hair like that, you should be wearing a gaggle of puppies on your back. Next time fix yourself up before you visit us." He ducked from the room before Sharon could slap him.

Kelsey removed her slacks and pulled on a miniskirt, trying to ignore Sharon's presence. But hands slithered around her waist. Sharon licked a wet path along her back.

"Why don't you let me lock the door and bring your heart rate up?"

Kelsey pushed her hands away. "I told you, I don't mix business with pleasure. You shouldn't have asked me to work here if you can't stick to the agreement."

"Then you're fired. I can't go another day without this luscious body."

Kelsey pulled away. "Sorry, boss. No can do."

"Is it because of that woman you went home with last night?"

"That's none of your business."

"Damn, sorry. Don't get your feathers ruffled." Sharon gave

her a gentle smile, then waved a yellow envelope. "This was waiting for you at the bar when I came out of my office."

Kelsey took the envelope, never turning her gaze from Sharon's bedroom eyes. "Thanks."

"You're welcome, sweet cheeks."

Sharon gave her a swat on the ass as she walked out the door. She was in love with Kelsey, poor thing. She'd been a great fuck, but love was far from Kelsey's mind where Sharon was concerned. Far from her mind, period. She should have stopped their fling a long time ago, before Sharon's heart became involved. Now she might have to consider quitting this job. It wasn't as if she really needed it, and she was fed up with the crowd at The Pink Lady; however, the freedom to play and have fun was worth the hassle. If she left, she would also miss the friends she had here.

Kelsey looked at the envelope. Only her name was written across the front. She tore open the edge and pulled out the contents, a note folded in half. Her heart attempted to tear its way through her chest as she read the message. Five typed words filled the page:

YOU ARE A DEAD BITCH.

Chapter Four

Kelsey let her gaze roam, seeking a hate-filled face. Though she tried not to think about the note, her mind kept wandering there anyway. A phone call she could dismiss as a disappointed drunk's idea of a joke. Maybe someone whose hands she'd brushed off thought it'd be funny to threaten her. But who would go to the trouble of delivering a note? That was another story.

She twirled around the pole and slipped to the floor, hands caressing the contours of her body, chest rising in the air, making the women scream louder. Thoughts of Jordan webbed through her mind with every inch her fingers traveled. She wanted Jordan's hands roaming the same path. She wanted Jordan's lips against hers and their bodies pressed so tight sweat couldn't invade their space.

The music ended. She plastered a fake smile on her face and studied the crowd again. Surely whoever wanted her dead would be here tonight to watch and wait for the perfect opportunity. Or perhaps the plan was to toy with her until she combusted with worry.

"I didn't see anyone," she said as she exited the stage.

Darren was also watching the frantic women from behind the curtain. He gave her a reassuring smile. "Probably a stupid joke."

"Yep. I'm sure it was."

One of the other dancers had called in sick, so Kelsey had another act before she could call it a night. She went in search of Sharon and found her curled in the chair at her computer.

"Are you sure you didn't see anyone drop off that letter?"

Sharon motioned her into the room. "I should have called you, but I was praying this would go away." She hesitated, as though she wasn't sure if she should speak. "I think whoever made the phone call is the same woman who left the letter. She called last night, too, right after you left."

Shocked, Kelsey echoed, "Last night? What did she say?"

"She made some threats against you and the woman you left with."

Fear spread through Kelsey like wildfire. "Why didn't you tell me?"

"I didn't want to scare you. I really thought it was just another sick joke." A concerned expression washed over her face. "But she called you by your real name."

Kelsey leaned against the wall for support. "Jesus, is she watching me?"

Sharon looked even more concerned. "I think you should come and stay with me for a few nights."

"I know how to defend myself, Sharon."

"I know you do, but I couldn't stand it if anything happened to you."

Kelsey's heart went out to her. She felt sorry for Sharon, but she didn't love her. And she didn't want to cause heartache by staying in her home like a regular guest when she knew Sharon would want more.

"I appreciate the offer, but I'll be fine."

Sharon shook her head. "You could let your new fuck fight your battle for you, I suppose."

Kelsey bit her tongue to keep from cussing her out. Without another word, she walked back to the bar and found an empty stool among the men who were now packed around the stage.

Darren breezed out from between the curtains, his boa flapping behind him. The men howled and slapped their hands on the floor, beckoning him to come their way. Someone slid in behind her. Kelsey half turned and met a pair of deep blue eyes. A heavily built woman with spiked blond hair nodded. Kelsey gave her a quick once-over, admiring her solid thighs and husky shoulders.

"He's fun to watch," the blonde said, voice deep and throaty.

"Yes, he is. Are you a fan?" Kelsey let her gaze fall between the woman's legs. You could never be too sure about some cross-dressers.

"A fan of fun people, but not a fan of men, if that's what you're asking."

Kelsey smiled. "Yep, I guess that's exactly what I was asking."

"I'm Paula." A wide hand inched out in front of her. "Nice to meet you."

Kelsey took the rough, calloused hand briefly. "I'm Veronica. Nice to meet you, too."

"Are you going to be dancing again?" The blue eyes flashed.

"Yes."

"Good, I can hardly wait."

To Kelsey's surprise, the blonde lifted her drink off the counter and walked away, taking a spot in the corner of the room. Kelsey's mind ran wild. Was she *the one*? Would the person who'd left the note have waltzed right up to her like that? The front door opened, blasting hot air into the room. Kelsey glanced over her shoulder and almost leaped to attention. Jordan stood in the doorway, her yummy body beckoning. Kelsey gripped the counter and their eyes met. A smile lifted the corners of Jordan's lickable lips. *Oh yeah, I've got to have another bite of that.*

Jordan squeezed through the crowd and took the stool beside her. "I wasn't sure whether to come back to this place or not."

"Why do you say that?" Kelsey thought about the lean stomach hidden under Jordan's pale blue shirt. She wanted to explore those hardened ridges again. And more.

Jordan shrugged. "To go or not to go—now, that's the question."

"You do what you want, baby. I'm here to dance, turn up the heat, send a few blood pressures sky-high." Kelsey gave her a wink. *Yours, especially.*

"Think we can have an encore of last night?"

Kelsey smiled. Her crotch heated automatically, bringing instant throbbing between her legs. "I think I can arrange that."

A loud slap on the counter sent her head whipping around.

"Time to shake that ass, sweetness." Sharon nodded toward the stage. "Let's go."

Jordan's jaw tightened for a split second, and Kelsey's heart raced wildly in her chest. She had the urge to slip her tongue in Jordan's mouth, to devour the taste of her toothpaste. Steadying her shaking hands, she slid off the stool. She didn't suffer from nerves before a routine, but knowing Jordan would be watching changed everything.

❖

Jordan instantly disliked the woman standing in front of her blocking her view of the stage.

"Hi. I'm Sharon Scott and I own this place. You want something to drink or what?"

"Beer."

Sharon slammed a bottle on the bar. "She's taken, you know." A snarl lifted her lips.

Jordan moved her gaze from the beer to the eyes filled with dislike. "Well," she eased off the stool, "someone might want to remind her of that."

She grabbed the neck of the bottle, slapped a five on the counter, and pushed through the crowd to find the perfect place to watch Kelsey's erotic dance. Her heart jumped as the lights dimmed and a delicious leg slithered through the curtain, straightening in the air. A hand joined the leg, sliding along the contours. The curtain flew back and Jordan's breath jammed in her throat.

Kelsey locked eyes with her as she advanced to the edge of the stage and sank slowly to her knees. Dollar bills were shoved in every free space available on her thong. That bitable ass rose in the air while her face rested on the floor. Jordan could think of a million things she wanted to do to that ass, that body, those lips...hell, every inch of firm, hot flesh. Her crotch soaked as those blue eyes bored through her. Kelsey gave her a seductive smile.

A burly woman with blond, spiked hair shoved her way through the screaming pack of dykes and femmes. The bouncer beside the stage blocked her approach. His dark skin glowed like burnished onyx under the stage lights. She slid a bill into his hand and said something. He folded the bill in half and waved to Kelsey, flashing the denomination. She nodded and the woman climbed onto the stage. The bouncer slid a chair after her.

Fire erupted inside Jordan as Kelsey pushed the blonde down in the chair, shoved a high heel into her chest, and dragged her fingers across her crotch. Beads of perspiration trickled down her spine when Kelsey followed the same seductive steps she'd taken in that back room. Slipping her hands inside the woman's shirt from behind, she roamed between her breasts and down over her stomach. She licked at the woman's ears while her fans screamed.

Jordan shifted in her chair. She was ready to rip both their heads off. It took every ounce of her self-control not to leap on the stage and drag Kelsey away. She glanced around at the women staring wild-eyed at the performance. When she looked back, Kelsey's sights were locked on her and she gave a saucy wink, letting Jordan know she wasn't forgotten.

Jordan stilled her pounding heart and gave her best smile,

though the jealous monster inside her still raged. She didn't really want to see what happened next, yet she couldn't look away. Kelsey moved in front of the woman. Facing the crowd, she bent her knees and hung her head, letting her hair fall to the stage like a curtain of spun gold. Then she slowly backed her fine ass onto the woman's lap, opened her legs for a straddle, and tossed her head back, spraying blond tentacles through the air. With her hips against the woman's stomach, she undulated, grinding in slow circles.

Jordan's blood pressure rose another notch when the woman's hands slithered between Kelsey's legs. Kelsey tossed them to the side and stood, shaking her head. Jordan smiled. This was her favorite part, watching the arrogant dancer tear down any opponent who dared to step on the mat with her.

When the song ended, the blonde followed Kelsey through the curtain. Seconds dragged by and Jordan tensed, not knowing what to do. Should she follow and ward off Kelsey's panting fan, or stay in her seat and let Kelsey take care of her own business? She was used to this. Right? But Jordan wasn't. She was seriously rethinking her need to come back here tonight when the curtain finally flapped open and the cross-dresser stuck his head through the folds.

"Harold, we need some help back here," he yelled to the bouncer by the stage.

Jordan shoved out of her chair, scrambled past the bouncer, and fought her way onto the stage. As she tore the curtain aside, she almost fell over the spike-haired blonde who'd paid for the public lap dance. She was sprawled on the floor like a discarded potato sack with Kelsey standing over her, a thin heel pressed firmly into her chest.

The bouncer bumped into Jordan, then busted out laughing as he looked to the floor. "Who needs a bouncer when we have Veronica?" He took the too-eager fan by the arm and hauled her up. "Come on. That's enough for tonight."

"You bitch!" the woman screamed at Kelsey.

Kelsey's gorgeous face contorted into anger as a look of realization darkened her eyes. "Are you the freak who left that nasty little letter?"

The blonde gave Kelsey an evil grin, and Jordan felt herself twitch, slipping into protective mode on impulse.

Harold steered the angry woman toward the door, using his broad chest as a barrier. "Outside," he snarled.

The woman gritted her teeth and raked her eyes over Kelsey's body. "Remember my face. One day, you'll see it again."

Chapter Five

"I swiped some information from your desperate fan," Harold said, joining the small group crowding Kelsey's dressing room.

"Did you get her full name?" Kelsey asked.

"Paula Riching."

Kelsey's breath caught. A name bounced into her mind. Riching Incorporated. How could she ever forget? Her father had died two weeks after that takeover. He'd worked himself into a heart attack.

"Dammit," she cursed. "I hate everything I'm doing right now. My job, my life...everything."

Sharon shoved around Jordan and hugged Kelsey. "It's okay, baby doll. Let me take you home and get you in the bath. You need some rest." She loosened her grip and held Kelsey at arm's length. "I don't want you stripping anymore. I can't take this."

Kelsey stared in amazement, waiting for her to turn into Emily Rose and need a priest. The hardcore businesswoman was suddenly behaving like a sappy, let–me–take–care–of–you girlfriend. "It's never bothered you before."

"Bullshit. I just wanted you to be happy. But I'm drawing the line now. I'll fire you if I have to."

"Whatever." Kelsey pulled away. "I think you've been in the liquor cabinet too long."

Jordan's worried green eyes were locked on her. "Is there something I should know? Who *was* that woman?"

"Who cares?" Kelsey found a pair of jeans and yanked them on, muttering, "Jeez, can't a girl get any privacy?"

No one made a move to leave.

Leaning back on the couch, Darren curled his legs under him. "Do you think she's the same person who left the death threat? She was pretty pissed at you."

"Death threat?" Jordan blazed with anger. "Someone threatened you?"

"We're taking care of the problem, aren't we, babe?" Sharon started patting Kelsey again and glared at Jordan, dislike etched on her face.

Kelsey slipped a pair of flip-flops onto her feet. "She seemed more interested in things other than slicing my throat."

She looked around. Darren, who couldn't fight to save his life, picked at his nails. Sharon, pretending they were the perfect couple, stared at Jordan as if she could rip her to shreds. Harold was ready for action...she needed only say the word. And Jordan looked just as dangerous.

"I have to think." Kelsey rubbed her temples.

"Let me get my things and we'll go." Sharon about tripped over her own feet heading for the door.

"I'm going home to my own place, Sharon." Kelsey met Jordan's eyes.

"You're not going home with *her*!" Sharon's lip curled. "You hardly know her. She's a stranger you picked up for a quick fuck."

Kelsey's anger flared. "Can you guys please excuse us for a second?" She gave everyone a cool glance. "Go. Now!"

"Holy Mother of God." Darren flew from the couch, dragging Jordan by the arm. "Run for your life."

Harold hurried out ahead, moving fast for a big guy. The door slammed shut behind them.

"Is everything okay?" Jordan asked as they hovered in the hallway.

"Shh. I just *love* their catfights." Darren pressed his ear to the door.

"She'll be fine," Harold said. "She knows her limits."

"That woman's not for you. She's not even your type," Sharon screamed loudly from behind the hollow door.

Jordan arched her eyebrows. "Do they do this often?"

"Nah," Darren said. "But they're *so* fun to watch."

"You don't know what my fucking type is," Kelsey yelled. "And you sure as hell don't tell me who I can and can't sleep with."

"Get away from that door, fool." Harold tugged at Darren's arm. "You can hear perfectly fine from here."

"You can't hear punches. I want to know when to call for an ambulance."

"Maybe I should leave," Jordan mumbled. Did they also have makeup sex after their fights?

"I want you back," Sharon continued. "And not just as an anytime fuck. I want more."

"Oh, shit." Darren covered his open mouth dramatically. "Call 911. She's touching."

"Get your damn hands off me." Kelsey's swift response echoed. "I don't love you. Don't make this any harder."

A long silence followed. Darren jammed his ear to the door.

"I'm only going to tell you one more time. Get your fucking hands off me."

Jordan's breath caught in her chest at Kelsey's steely voice. She meant business.

"She's going to spare the boss's life." Darren slapped his hands together and looked to the ceiling. "Thank you, God, fashion gods, Mother Mary, and…fuck, all of you up there. I need my paycheck today."

"Fine, go ruin your life. Like it's not screwed up enough

already. And now your enemies are breathing down your neck. Just get out of here."

Darren backed away, whistling a pathetic imitation of *The Andy Griffith Show* theme song as the door opened.

Kelsey's face was contorted in anger. She stared from one of her friends to the next, finally settling on Jordan. "Let's go!"

Jordan had never been one to take orders well, but she found herself following Kelsey anyway. A cool night breeze whipped through her hair, doing absolutely nothing to lower the heat coming to a slow boil between her legs. Tonight's reprise had sent her pulse rocketing, and take-charge Kelsey was an added bonus.

"She makes me so damn mad." Kelsey kicked the ground, spraying pebbles across the parking lot.

"So I heard." Jordan shrugged when Kelsey looked up. "Thin walls."

"Yeah."

"I know the perfect place we can go to get you under control. You game?"

Kelsey grinned. "Will it include a bed?"

"Nope. But it will include soft mats."

"Lead the way."

❖

"Jordan's House of Karate." Kelsey raised her eyebrows. "I'm impressed."

"Thank you." Pride washed over Jordan. She never realized having someone else appreciate what she did for a living would be so gratifying, but the feeling spreading through her gut was well worth the stress of the evening. She locked the door behind them and fanned out a hand. "Welcome to my home away from home."

Kelsey took in the framed pictures and stopped to read the trophies. "Wow. You've won some mighty fine titles."

Jordan bowed.

"That must be an awesome feeling." Kelsey crossed to a glass case holding different colored belts, then walked along another open shelf lined with trophies. Her fingers trailed over a figurine.

Jordan envisioned those fingers trailing along her skin in the same gentle caress. Her crotch burned.

"So, you said something about me getting some frustrations out." Kelsey yanked her from her fantasy.

"Yes. Follow me." Jordan led her into the locker room and tossed her a pair of workout pants. "Here. Put these on."

Instead of escaping into a private cubicle, Kelsey gave Jordan a hot smile and unsnapped her jeans. She slid them down slowly, rolling her hips. A white lace thong screamed for Jordan to remove it. She was unable to look away from the tempting curves while Kelsey finished changing.

"Ready?" Kelsey asked with an amused smile.

Jordan's lungs had ceased to expand. Heat prickled along her skin.

"Stretch," she mumbled. It was the nicest command she could think of when all she wanted to do was ram her fingers inside Kelsey and make her scream with satisfaction.

"Yes, ma'am." Kelsey saluted, slipped to the floor, pulled her legs together, and hung over them. She slowly slid her legs apart in a split and lay flat on the floor, cheek kissing the mat.

Oh, Jesus, give me strength.

"Up," Jordan demanded before she ran out of self-control. She pulled thick pads over her hands. "Punch. Hard. Until you feel better."

"You're kidding, right?"

"Why would I be? This'll make you feel better. You can take your anger out on me."

Kelsey hung her head, shaking it back and forth. Long strands escaped her hair clip.

"What?" Jordan asked, confused.

"You're not the smartest cookie on the farm, are you?"

Jordan offered a padded hand. "Watch it, woman."

With a patient smile, Kelsey prompted, "Did you notice what happened to that weirdo at the club?"

"You think you can flatten me with a lucky punch?" Jordan laughed.

"Okay, put 'em up." Kelsey lifted her hands defensively in front of her face.

Jordan did as commanded. She wanted to alleviate Kelsey's anger, then make love to her, right here on this floor. She wanted to trace every curve of her body and hear her cries of pleasure.

"Good," she said as Kelsey landed a soft punch. "Now harder, until you feel your anger draining. Don't hold back."

"I wouldn't have it any other way." Kelsey punched harder, jabbing her delicate hands one after the other into the pads.

"Wow. You look like a natural. Feeling better?"

"Not really, but this is fun. When do we get on with the real stuff?"

"Real stuff?"

Kelsey gave a punch that would have driven any opponent to their knees, then dropped to the floor and swiped Jordan's feet out from under her. She landed on her side with a grunt, instinctively breaking her fall. Kelsey pushed her over onto her back and straddled her, pinning her arms above her head. She eased the pads off Jordan's hands and tossed them aside.

"Tae Kwon Do." Cinnamon breath feathered across Jordan's face. With a sweet smile, Kelsey added, "Never underestimate your opponent."

Jordan stared up at her in disbelief. Desire flowed through every vein in her body. Her breath hitched and goose bumps trailed her skin.

I'm going to fuck her brains out.

❖

Kelsey stared into the most beautiful eyes she'd ever seen. The look of complete surprise on Jordan's face made her feel so warm she wanted to claw at her skin. Too bad Jordan was only a fuck. She could see herself settling down with someone just like her, someone kind and considerate, yet stony hard and incredible between the sheets.

"Come here." Jordan's kissable mouth moved in a seductive whisper.

Kelsey leaned in until she found the hot lips and a tongue snaked into her mouth. She moaned while she sucked at Jordan's soft tongue, trailing her fingers through her silken hair. Jordan rolled her over and kneed her legs apart. Her fingers followed close behind, inching across Kelsey's crotch, burning a path of fire. Jordan's lips moved to her neck, kissing a wet track across her skin.

"I've thought about fucking you all day," she mumbled.

Her gaze made Kelsey feel like a gleaming masterpiece in an art gallery. "Don't talk." She placed her finger over Jordan's lips. "Just do it."

She closed her eyes as Jordan scooped her hand around to her ass and dragged the pants and thong off her body. The halter top was next. Straddling her from beneath, Kelsey draped her arms around her neck and ground her hips into Jordan's hard stomach, wanting and needing an orgasm. Her breath hitched when Jordan's fingers slipped between her legs. Out of her mind with insatiable urgency, she sucked in a deep breath as her clit surged against Jordan's fingers. The slow circling wasn't enough. She bore down hard and let her head fall back.

Jordan didn't tease her this time. She seemed to know exactly what Kelsey needed. And how to deliver it.

Chapter Six

Jordan held Kelsey while she quivered in her arms. She wanted to hold her forever. The way her body responded was breathtaking. With her face against Kelsey's chest, she breathed in her sweet, floral scent mixed with sexy pheromones. She circled her finger faster on Kelsey's clit, matching the rhythm of her grinding hips. Kelsey's body went rigid right before she released a low moan. Jordan slipped her hand farther down, then drilled her fingers inside.

Kelsey whipped her head from side to side, circling her pussy over Jordan's hand, sharp cries escaping her throat. It was the most beautiful sound Jordan had ever heard. She expected a writhing body, more hair pulling. Instead, Kelsey wrapped her arms around her neck, holding onto her like a life preserver. She entwined her hands in Jordan's hair and rocked against her, humping steadily over her thrusting fingers. Moans filled the room and Kelsey shook like a tree in the middle of a fierce storm. Jordan shoved her fingers up as hard and far as she could while the walls of Kelsey's insides clenched in vise-grip waves.

Too soon her orgasm diminished, calming to light pulses, and she sagged in Jordan's arms. Jordan withdrew her fingers and held her close. They lay still for what felt like eternity, neither speaking nor attempting to move. Kelsey finally rolled out of Jordan's lap and they both sat up.

Jordan stroked the curls that escaped Kelsey's hair clip. "You game for dinner, a movie…more fucking?"

Kelsey gave her a gentle smile. "You're not seriously asking me out on a date, are you?"

Jordan shrugged. "Not really. I like movies and dinner. And fucking."

"Good. For a minute there, I thought you were going to go all mushy on me." Kelsey pulled out of her grasp and slipped into her clothes.

Jordan stilled the impulse to fling her back to the floor and fuck her until she screamed for mercy. Instead, she got to her feet and started for the door. Kelsey grabbed her arm and she turned, not wanting to look back into those seductive blue eyes.

"Jordan, I also like movies and dinner. And fucking."

❖

A whirlpool of confusion spiraled through Kelsey. Her life, her career, her now two-time fuck partner, Jordan. Then there was Paula Riching and whoever wanted Kelsey dead—the stress was enough to make her want to hide. Her job at Billings Industries was sucking her soul away, and yet being with Jordan made her think of nothing, not even the possibility that tomorrow could be her last breath, her last sale, or her last dance.

Jordan's lean back and the strong curves of her tight buttocks mesmerized Kelsey as they walked to the front of the karate shop. Jordan lived her whole life for the next win, just like Kelsey lived hers for the next business slaughter. Maybe destiny had brought them together. Kelsey sucked in a breath and focused on the gold pieces hogging the space on the white walls. An image of her office came to mind, with her awards and accomplishments framed around the room. Were she and Jordan so different? She ripped apart lives like Jordan ripped apart heads.

Jordan locked the front doors and they strolled to the Viper. "Where to, my lady?"

"I dunno. What type of food do you like?"

Jordan wiggled her eyebrows and glanced down at Kelsey's crotch.

Kelsey grimaced playfully. "Be serious."

"I was. I like just about anything as long as it's not crawling across my plate." She stepped around Kelsey to open the passenger door.

Kelsey acknowledged the gentlemanly courtesy with a smile, and slipped onto the leather seat. "I'm a steak lover," she said once Jordan had settled and started the engine.

"Steak it is."

They pulled out of the parking lot and eased into traffic. A crisp night wind blew through the windows, doing little to help the prickle of goose bumps traveling along Kelsey's arms. Bright lights from the storefronts flashed across her eyes as Jordan wove through traffic. They soon arrived at the restaurant and found a booth. The server introduced herself and took their order.

"How long have you owned the karate shop?" Kelsey spoke just to hear something other than her own breathing. Was the conversation strained because they both knew their connection linked only to the bedroom?

"Almost ten years." Jordan smiled.

"And you train as well?"

"As much as my body can handle. I have two assistants, but I'm always there."

The waitress returned with their drinks and a loaf of rye bread on a wooden platter. Kelsey leaned back to stare at Jordan. God, she seemed so calm. Maybe that's what the attraction was. Amidst the chaos of Kelsey's life, Jordan was the eye of a hurricane, smooth and gentle, while the outer winds heaved in turmoil.

Jordan's arms rested on the edge of the table. A muscle tweaked while she played with the utensils rolled inside her napkin. "I'm curious. How'd you get into Tae Kwon Do?"

Kelsey sighed, her mind flooding with memories of training. "An overprotective father, I guess."

"Do you do anything other than dance at The Pink Lady?"

Kelsey nodded. "I run my father's business." She liked saying those words sometimes. Most women found it cool that she could wield power in a man's world. That was, until they found out exactly what that man's world consisted of. "He died almost two years ago."

"I'm sorry to hear that." Sympathy was razor sharp in Jordan's eyes. She obviously wanted to ask more questions but sensed the topic was difficult.

Kelsey suddenly felt the urge to tell her about the fucked-up Billings family. How her worthless brother behaved and how her mom had given up on her marriage and abandoned her kids as teenagers for reasons Kelsey was never sure about. She missed her, especially now that she was in the process of changing the company. Perhaps her mother would be proud of her. Kelsey vaguely recalled her parents quarreling over John Billings's obsession with the business.

The waitress arrived with their dinner and they ate in silence. Jordan gave off an aura of protection, of security. Kelsey wanted to feel those strong arms wrap around her again. This affair would have to come to a halt very soon. Her privacy depended on it. But in the meantime, she intended to enjoy every moment. It was unusual for her to want more from a woman than her body. Maybe she just felt vulnerable because her life wasn't quite going to plan. Kelsey frowned as a feeling stirred deep inside. She stared down at her meal, recognizing the dull ache even as she stomped it down. Loneliness.

Watching a shadow pass across Kelsey's face, Jordan stilled the impulse to reach for her hand. If they were alone, she'd strip off her clothes, throw warm blankets around them, and drift off to sleep, skin on skin. There was something about Kelsey that screamed secrets, that begged for protection. But they weren't alone. They were in public, where people gawked and sometimes made rude comments to lesbians who showed affection.

"Are you okay?" Jordan asked, searching Kelsey's face.

"I'm fine." Kelsey looked past her with an unreadable expression. She pointed to an infant cradled in her mother's arms two booths over. "She's so cute. And so tiny."

Jordan felt her heartstrings react. Did Kelsey even like babies? Or kids? She didn't know anything about the woman who intrigued her, except that her life seemed drenched in drama. The realization that she cared was like a smack to the face. Where were these emotions coming from? Hadn't she been desperate to keep her freedom once she had it again? For some damn reason, she wanted to know Kelsey's hopes and dreams and secrets, her wishes and desires. She wanted to find out everything about her, no matter how bad, small, or dramatic.

"Let's get out of here," she said.

"I thought you'd never ask." Kelsey slid out of the booth.

Jordan tossed bills on the table to cover the tab and tip. They walked along the street in silence. She felt uneasy as they got into the car. Something was different. They'd just had great sex and she knew they were going back to Kelsey's place to spend the night together. She glanced sideways at Kelsey, thinking about the fight with Sharon. Kelsey was obviously allergic to women who tried to own her. That was something they had in common.

Jordan drove automatically until she reached the freeway exit into Kelsey's neighborhood. She'd almost decided to make some excuse and go home when she saw the familiar gates. She keyed in the code Kelsey gave her and parked in front of the house. As the engine died, a fire ignited inside her, removing all doubt as to what they would be doing all night. She wanted to throw the seat back and start making love right here in the driveway.

Letting out her breath, she followed Kelsey indoors and along a wide hallway to her bedroom. Faint light stretched across the room from the full moon. As soon as they neared the bed, fingers started working, yanking and tugging clothes from their bodies until they fell naked onto the bed. Their lips locked, tongues dancing. Hands searched and explored. Kelsey pushed Jordan onto her back and straddled her hips. She opened a drawer on the nightstand and pulled out a hot pink vibrator. Moonlight glimmered off the shiny plastic.

White heat flared between Jordan's legs. With a playful grin, she took the device from Kelsey and twisted the end until vibrations tingled her palm.

"I assume you want me to use this?" She tossed Kelsey onto the sheets and pried her legs open with a knee.

Kelsey caged her between her thighs and gave her a sinful smile. "Who said I wanted it for me?"

Jordan licked her way across Kelsey's chest, inches from her hardened nipple. "I'm better at giving than receiving."

Kelsey wriggled. "Then give it to me." She rubbed her crotch against Jordan's pelvis.

Jordan smiled and pulled free of the vise grip. She shimmied down, licking a wet trail to Kelsey's pert nipples. Eagerly, she slipped one tip between her lips, then the other, before moving down to dip her tongue in Kelsey's belly button. Finally, she lowered herself until she was face-to-face with her new lover's slick opening.

Kelsey's breathing was already abnormal with anticipation. She exhaled raggedly, releasing a low groan as Jordan laid the humming device under her. Slowly Jordan inserted the vibrator. Kelsey bucked, matching each long, slippery stroke. As she thrust, Jordan nursed eagerly on her clit.

When her panting grew hard, Jordan could take no more. She wanted this quivering body wrapped tight in her arms when Kelsey's orgasm coursed through her. She released her clit, and rose above her.

Kelsey huffed. "Don't stop."

Pinning her arms above her head, Jordan lay on top of her and drove the vibe skillfully, holding it trapped between her thighs. Kelsey draped her legs over Jordan, locking her feet around Jordan's back. Jordan clamped her lips on Kelsey's and sucked the tip of her tongue into her mouth. With every pump of her hips the vibrator rubbed against her clit, making her ache for release.

Kelsey matched her, stroke for stroke, spiraling Jordan's orgasm closer to the brink. Soft cries penetrated the night. Kelsey bucked harder and faster, driving her pussy over the vibrator.

"Oh, my God. Oh…" she screamed, her hips thrusting wildly under Jordan's weight.

Jordan released her wrists and Kelsey's arms flew around her neck while her body froze. Her erotic mewing was too much. Jordan's orgasm ricocheted through her as Kelsey shuddered and let out her own passionate, pent-up moan. Quivering, Jordan fell against her and nuzzled her face into her neck, breathing in her sweaty scent. Kelsey's fingers trailed along her back and spine.

They lay in their sweaty tangle until their breathing slowed, then Jordan tossed the vibe on the floor and rolled onto her back next to Kelsey. Her heart skipped erratically at the confusion rushing through her veins. Emotions bubbled up and words threatened to spill from her lips. She wasn't even sure what she wanted to say. She waited for some sign that Kelsey might feel as stunned as she did, but no hand reached for hers. There was no kiss. Sadly, whatever she felt would be hidden from Kelsey forever.

Kelsey didn't have to say the words that Jordan was nothing more than a fuck. Jordan heard the message, loud and clear.

❖

Some time later, Kelsey combed her fingers through Jordan's short hair and breathed in her sweet smell. Soon, they'd both resume their normal lives, Jordan and her karate, she and her company. More than likely, they'd never see each other again. She meant to hang on to this night for as long as she could. She deserved some tranquility, if only for a short time.

Jordan shifted and nuzzled her face deeper into Kelsey's neck. "That was awesome."

Kelsey agreed. Even the word "awesome" wasn't glorious enough to describe how powerful it had been. "You're a great lover."

She wanted to call the comment back as soon as it slipped out. Telling someone they were a great lover gave them power. She didn't want Jordan to have any more control than she did already.

Jordan leaned on her elbow, trailing soft fingers between Kelsey's breasts before letting them come to rest on her stomach. "Coming from you, I take that as a huge compliment."

Kelsey wouldn't admit that not a single lover had ever made her feel like she was floating on a cloud hours after making love. "Come on. Let's go watch a movie."

She gave Jordan a quick peck on the cheek and slid out of bed. She retrieved the vibrator, scrubbed it clean in the bathroom, and then returned it to the drawer. With luck, they'd use it again before the night was over. Her eyes strayed to Jordan, who stood by the bed, her naked body demanding attention. Her lean stomach and tight muscular legs were a spectacular combination. God, how Kelsey wanted to feel her tongue travel over every inch of this woman.

Jordan caught her arm, pulling her into an embrace, and her lips clamped over Kelsey's. Heat splashed between Kelsey's legs with lightning speed. How was this possible after the earthquake only minutes before? Her knees weakened and she playfully pushed Jordan away before she gave in.

Refusing to let her dictate when they would make love again, she said, "If you don't stop, we're never going to make it out of this bedroom."

"You say that like it's a problem."

Kelsey didn't answer. It would only be a problem if she let their fling continue, and that wasn't going to happen. She found them boxers and T-shirts and, after dressing, they went into the living room and plopped onto the couch. With a movie rolling across the TV screen, they snuggled under blankets.

Kelsey had never felt so peaceful. She couldn't remember the last time she'd cuddled in front of the television with someone, if she ever had. It wasn't really her style, but she felt incredibly content.

When the movie was over, they crept back in bed. This time they removed their clothing with slow, steady fingers. They had the rest of the night, and Kelsey knew the memories would forever burn in her mind.

❖

Kelsey opened her eyes and stretched. The warm body next to hers was gone, leaving emptiness. Even in her lonely world, she could never remember a time when she'd felt this type of void. She had meant to say good-bye before Jordan left, but in a way she was glad they didn't have to do that. She wasn't sure if she could fake her usual blasé attitude, and if Jordan read her true feelings in her eyes, things could get complicated.

She dragged herself to the bathroom and cleaned her teeth. As she got back into bed, a delicious aroma teased her senses. Coffee? While she was still processing the unsettling idea, the door opened and Jordan strolled into the room with a mug in her hand.

"I didn't know how you like yours, so I loaded it up with sugar and cream."

Kelsey sat up against the headboard and accepted the coffee. Eyeing Jordan cautiously, she took a sip, and groaned as the delicious taste filled her mouth. "It's wonderful. Thank you."

"You're welcome. Breakfast will be ready in about ten minutes." She left the room.

Kelsey stared after her. Had a lover ever served her breakfast? Hell, she'd never allowed anyone besides Sharon to stay after the fuck was over. The other women she'd brought home asked way too many questions and left her no choice but to send them on their merry way.

She was shocked that Jordan was still here. She had the impression freedom meant a lot to her, too. Jordan was a strong woman. She didn't need to cling to someone she could look up to, or make compromises because she didn't feel complete without a girlfriend. She was the kind of person who could probably understand why Kelsey held on to her father's company with a strong grip.

Kelsey shook the unrealistic thought from her mind. People only saw her as a corporate raider, not a caring person. No one knew yet that she was trying to find a way to change the company and still make profits. No one would ever truly understand that her love for her father had forced her to endure and continue his legacy. He'd loved the company more than anything. Even after her mother pleaded and threatened to leave, he'd continued holding tight to his monster's reins.

That empire was Kelsey's now, and she couldn't look down her nose at him for creating it. If she had to live the rest of her life alone, then so be it. Her father had taught her everything she knew, how to be strong and independent and to stand up for what she believed in. She couldn't let him down by running away from the empire he'd sacrificed so much to build.

She slid out of bed, pulled on boxers and a T-shirt, and headed to the kitchen.

"It smells good in here." She eyed the sandwiches of bacon, eggs, lettuce, and thin slices of tomato that Jordan had arranged on plates. Her mouth watered.

Jordan placed a sandwich in front of her and sat on the other stool. "I figured we'd worked up quite an appetite."

Just thinking about the things they'd done throughout the night made Kelsey shudder. Jordan had ripped multiple orgasms from her, leaving her breathless and sated before they finally drifted off to sleep. She shifted her attention to her sandwich, taking determined bites.

"Do you have plans today?" Jordan asked.

Kelsey glanced at the clock above the sink. "I have to get to work."

"What about tonight?"

Stretching their liaison out would only lead to disclosures Kelsey didn't want to make. Ending this before it could get too far was the only way around her dilemma.

"Sorry. Got plans," she lied.

Jordan nodded and bit into her sandwich. Disappointment splashed her eyes. Kelsey's heart pounded. How could one more night hurt? She didn't have to tell Jordan everything. She consumed some more of her sandwich while she tried to firm up her resolve. How many encounters did it take before a fling became a relationship? She never let anyone stay in her life long enough to find out.

Jordan wasn't giving up easily. Her eyes glittered, daring Kelsey to say yes. "Tomorrow?"

Kelsey hesitated, torn between logic and lust. "I'll be free around three, after my lunch meeting."

Jordan grinned. "I'll pick you up at three thirty."

Kelsey perked a brow. "Who said you could?"

"I did." Jordan gave her a bright smile and carried their empty plates to the sink.

Kelsey could have kicked herself as she watched her rinse the dishes. She was asking for trouble. The best idea would be to call Jordan tomorrow afternoon and cancel. She could say good-bye over the phone. She couldn't slow her heart down as Jordan crossed the room toward her and eased between her legs.

"You ready for a shower?" Jordan's smile deepened into mischief. "I have a few areas to clean."

Chapter Seven

Rap music drifted from open apartments as Jordan tapped on her mother's door. An image of Kelsey grinding to that hard beat slid into her mind. Her mom slipped the curtain back, gave her a frown, and then unlocked various chains and bolts.

"Is something wrong?" she asked as Jordan strolled into the tiny space.

"No. Can't a daughter visit her mother?"

"Are you getting sassy with me, young lady?" She led Jordan to the kitchen where a bowl of beef stew waited. "Want some of my homemade stew?"

"No, thanks. I'll have a late lunch when I get back to work."

Her stomach gave a low grumble of protest. There was nothing in the world like her mother's home-cooked meals, especially her stew. Yet if Jordan wasn't allowed to buy groceries, she would be damned if she'd eat and deprive her mom of a second serving.

"You're too skinny. You need to eat." Susan Porter's weary gaze roamed over her. "You look…different. Same rosy cheeks and bright eyes, but there's something…" Her fingers flew to her mouth. "Is my baby in love?"

Jordan cringed. Where she was concerned, her mother's

imagination ran wild. She couldn't wait to have grandchildren and was always looking for clues that Jordan was ready to settle down.

"Jeez, Mom. I'm not in love. I just came to see how you were doing."

"What's her name? Does she like kids?"

Immediate suffocation cramped Jordan's chest. Leave it to her mom to become nosey. "There's no *she*."

"You didn't say if she liked kids. She has to love kids. I want to be a grandma, remember."

"Mom, you're not listening to me."

"She loves kids. Excellent."

Jordan dropped into a chair. "Why are you so hardheaded?"

Her mother walked over to the table and set down a glass of tea. "God made me that way. He made you that way, too. That's why you're not telling me about her. But it's okay if you want to keep her a secret. I understand."

Jordan rolled her eyes. She grabbed the glass and took a long swig, praying the ice-cold fluid would cool off her hot thoughts. Was she in love? Was her mother's intuition correct? No. Her freedom was too precious. And besides, she and Kelsey had only met a couple of days ago.

"Tell me where your last match is going to be. Can I come and watch? You have no idea how excited I am that you won't be hurting your body anymore."

Here we go again. Jordan was shocked at the thought that her final competition was approaching. When had she decided not to fight again? And why? Competing was the only thing that truly made her happy. Was that happiness fading away? Or was the reason she wanted to compete fading away?

Showing people how strong she was had always been important to her. In this world, lesbians were shunned. Though times were changing, coming out of the closet in her high school days had put her on guard. Yet a need to feel safe and in control was not her only reason for fighting. Winning matches gave her a thrill beyond description, a heated rush that nothing else could match. Except, perhaps, making love with Kelsey.

"You've already beaten the crap out of everyone, so why keep putting yourself at risk?" her mother continued. "You've won your fair share of awards and those thingamabobs."

"Trophies?" Jordan arched her brow.

"No, honey. I'm not senile. Those pretty ones I like."

"Medallions?"

Her mother snapped her fingers, vigorously nodding. "Yes. Those. I love those. Anyway, as I was saying. I think it's good that you've finally got your priorities sorted out."

Jordan didn't respond. Had her mother truly ever praised her for her triumphs—for owning a successful business and winning every title she had competed for in the past ten years? Was she ashamed that her daughter was a lesbian, that she might never have grandchildren with her blood running through their veins? It saddened her that her mother wanted nothing more than to be a grandmother. No other accomplishment seemed to matter in her eyes.

"Maybe your lady friend will come to the match, too."

"I doubt that," Jordan said.

"So there *is* someone. I knew it."

Jordan sat the glass down and rose. "I'm going. Do you need anything?"

"No, sweetie. And please, stop worrying about me so much. You have more things to concern yourself with than me. Look." She flicked her hand around the sparsely decorated room. "I'm fine. Bills are paid, food on the table, phone to chat on. I'm doing great."

Jordan cringed. What a lie. Her mother had loved the spacious home she'd designed and decorated every inch of, the one she'd had to sell in this terrible real estate market to pay off her bills when the lab closed. Or rather, when the new owner swooped down and kicked out all the employees because the business had to be "restructured." Even the pension plan wasn't safe. The former employees were still fighting a legal battle to preserve their entitlements.

Jordan gritted her teeth. She'd give anything to get her hands on the fat cats who had bought and sold the business. They were the ones who were at fault here. They were the reason her mother was living in the projects, scraping to find the money for food. She wanted to see them rotting in hell. How could people be so greedy and heartless?

She kissed her mother's cheek. "If you need anything, just call. I mean it. Anything, anytime, anywhere. You're my mother and I love you."

"I will, baby." Sadness clouded her sweet face. "I love you, too."

Jordan knew she wouldn't call. She was too proud. Jordan knew someone else just like her.

Herself.

Feeling restless, she drove back to the karate shop to pick up some paperwork. Today was the quietest of her week and she wanted to spend the time catching up on her accounts and records. She didn't know how she was going to concentrate. Ever since she'd left Kelsey's place the day before, all she could think about was feeling her shivering climax and hearing her soft cries.

As she idled in a long line of traffic at a red light, she thought about calling off tonight's date. It was a mistake to keep seeing Kelsey. Jordan knew where this was going. She already found her irresistible and couldn't pretend it would be easy to walk away. How much power did she want to give up? Kelsey was a free bird. If Jordan tried to change that, she would be discarded, like Sharon.

She moved forward a few yards as the lights changed. A woman in a business suit caught her attention. She was seated outside at a corner café. Her hair was pinned into a messy bun, though lone strands framed her face. Black slacks wrapped slender legs, and a white blouse, three buttons undone, displayed killer cleavage. Images of Kelsey flashed into Jordan's mind. She shook her head, trying to swipe clean the memory of slender fingers sliding into her. If she cancelled their date, she'd probably never see Kelsey again, never have another chance to fuck her.

The woman at the table turned to a handsome man. Tall and dark haired, also wearing a business suit, he smiled and leaned into her. A pang gripped Jordan's gut. A serious expression altered the woman's profile, reminding Jordan of the hard glare Kelsey gave her in the back room.

A horn blasted behind her. She jerked forward, catching a full view of the woman. Holy shit. Jordan had to brake to avoid rear-ending the car ahead. The gorgeous woman was Kelsey. It wasn't like Jordan had never seen a woman go from jeans and T-shirt to totally classy chic. But Kelsey was different. She looked completely professional, like she'd been doing it for years. Like this was who she really was, and the stripper Jordan knew was just a fantasy.

Now she understood why Kelsey didn't "date." She led a double life, and the two halves did not overlap. Jordan thought about the threatening phone calls. Had someone from Kelsey's real life stumbled onto her other existence at The Pink Lady? Did she have an angry real-life girlfriend who had discovered that she fucked strangers she picked up in bars?

Jordan's hands shook on the steering wheel. She didn't know why she was so upset at the thought. Kelsey had a right to her privacy and her fantasies. Jordan had been a willing participant. No one had made any promises.

She stared straight ahead. What to do?

❖

After catching up on contracts and finalizing the due diligence for their latest takeover, Kelsey swiveled her chair to look out the window. The sky was dotted with white, puffy clouds and the day seemed to be dragging on forever. She still had three hours to wait and she yearned for Jordan's touch. Since when had she thought about a woman for longer than a few hours after hot sex? She couldn't remember one occasion, and she didn't want to start with Jordan.

Sighing, she paged Douglas. It was time to put their plans into motion. Hopefully, he would accept her change of mind. The decision to sell would be a shock, but she was sure he would help her find someone capable of taking over. When the door opened, admitting his tall, lean frame, she swallowed the lump forming in her throat. His crisp white shirt was unbuttoned at the collar, indicating he'd been frazzled over something. She smiled, envisioning him yanking open the button at his neck and forking his fingers through his hair, huffing over some contract document.

"What's up?" He eased into the chair across from her desk.

Kelsey met his gaze with determination. She trusted him. She knew he'd do everything possible to make sure this company fell into the right hands. "I really have decided to sell."

He blinked. "You're not serious. I thought you were just blowing off steam the other day."

She nodded. "Yep. Serious as can be."

The muscles in his neck tightened. "What about all the plans we've made? Are you just going to throw everything away?"

"I'm still going through with our plans, just letting someone else implement the changes."

Douglas leaned forward. "Listen to me. It doesn't matter what you want. If you honestly think someone is going to buy this company, then completely change its role, you're sadly mistaken. Billings has already built its reputation. That's what everyone wants. Not this flip of the coin you have in mind."

Kelsey let his words loll in her head. Was he correct? Would any buyer want a company that did little more than help struggling businesses? They'd want a tiger on the prowl...exactly what Billings Industries was now.

She propped her elbow on the desk and rested her chin against her fist. "I'll make it work. Somehow, some way. I'll make sure this company falls into the right hands."

Douglas stood abruptly. "I'm not going to talk to you about this right now. I don't know what's gotten into you, but you're not making rational decisions." He strode to the door and then paused, looking back at her with a mixture of bewilderment and sorrow. "We've spent entirely too much time on this. If you screw up, you'll live to regret it."

"I'm not going to screw up," Kelsey said. "You forget, I've been doing this for most of my life. I know how to make a deal."

"I think you're the one forgetting the past," Douglas replied. "Your father gave up a lot to make this company into what it is today. I know you, and you would never forgive yourself if you destroyed everything that mattered to him. Find me when you have your head back on straight."

He left the room before she could respond. Staring at the closed door, she wondered if he was right. She wasn't sure it was a chance she was willing to take, now that Douglas had thrown the ball back into her court. Owning this company, having it suck her life away, might not be what she wanted, but watching it disintegrate or degenerate wasn't something she could handle, either.

She rubbed her fingers against her temple. "If I could get her ass out of my head, maybe I *could* think straight."

This was ridiculous. She'd never thought she'd turn into a weak, pathetic, lust-struck fool, but she had. She checked her watch. Almost time to leave. She wondered what Jordan was doing right now. Was she getting ready for their evening or was she still training? Kelsey envisioned sweat rolling down her face and neck, pooling between her breasts. Had Jordan been thinking about her, too? She had a mental image of the delicate crease across her strong brow and the dreamy look that softened her eyes to a mysterious shade of jade.

"Fuck." She slammed out of her chair, wishing she'd never suggested they meet up again.

She had to do something to get her mind back where it needed to be—away from Jordan. Dancing usually cleared her head and calmed her emotions, but that wasn't an option. Tonight belonged to her and Jordan, and it would be the last evening they shared. Kelsey promised herself she would make it one they would both remember when they went their separate ways.

❖

"Damn, you look good enough to eat. Literally."

Jordan's gaze gobbled up every inch of her, making Kelsey feel like Cinderella heading to the ball. Her low-cut blue jeans and burgundy silk shirt sure didn't fit the attire of a princess. And the flip-flops and silver toe rings weren't glass slippers. Yet Jordan's intense stare made her feel precious.

Kelsey smiled. "You never said where we were going, so I didn't know what to wear."

"I like the naked look, myself," Jordan teased. "But I'd rather not get us arrested."

She stepped onto the porch, stopping Kelsey's heart. Her dark carpenter jeans catered to her lean thighs. A pale yellow shirt was tucked inside her waistband, begging Kelsey to find the goodies hidden beneath. She imagined kneeling between her naked thighs and slurping until a scream rumbled through her.

Jordan's gaze dipped to Kelsey's lips and she closed the gap between them, gently joining their mouths. Fire banged like a pinball through Kelsey's insides and settled between her legs. Jordan pulled back with a grunt of reluctance.

"Your chariot awaits, my lovely." She waved toward the car.

Kelsey chuckled and walked ahead of her to the Viper. Jordan grabbed the handle before she could open the door. Kelsey wanted to point out that she wasn't really into the gallant-knight stuff, but the look of contentment on Jordan's face stopped her. She held her gaze and consumed every laugh line, feeling her heart pound harder. Jordan smelled delicious, too, soft traces of citrus blending with spice. Quickly, Kelsey slid onto the seat before she changed her mind and dragged Jordan inside the house. She had a feeling, from the look of desire on Jordan's face, that she wouldn't put up a fight.

Jordan sucked in a deep breath as she started the car and pulled through the gate. Would Kelsey laugh at her romantic plans? She was about to find out. She wasn't sure what possessed her, but she reached over and covered Kelsey's hand with her own. The contact felt like the most natural thing in the world. Wanting more, she almost stroked Kelsey's cheek in affection. If she didn't stop these little gestures of romance, she was going to find her heart in a meat grinder.

"How was your day?" she asked.

Kelsey tensed. "Don't let's talk about our jobs." Her tone was suddenly frigid. "Jobs are so boring."

Jordan could have argued, but she didn't want to waste precious time. She knew Kelsey wasn't happy in her day job and could read between the lines. The suit she'd seen her wearing earlier looked expensive and conservative, the kind of outfit women wore when they wanted respect from male peers. She'd said she ran her father's business and Jordan had imagined a family concern, something modest and certainly not very profitable. Why else would she have a second job stripping? But it looked like she was involved in the corporate world as well, probably in one of those high-powered jobs where less-qualified men still called the shots. That would make anyone ambivalent.

"What would you like to talk about?" Jordan asked.

Kelsey pulled her hand free. "We don't have to talk about anything at all."

True. Very true. Getting to know each other would only leave extra memories lingering when this one-night stand—hell, Jordan wasn't sure what to call it—was over. She'd sworn she would walk away after tonight, but the more she was with Kelsey, the more she wanted to see her again. Tonight had to be the last time. She intended to walk away with her head held high in the morning.

She guided the car to the curb at the entrance to a city park and said, "Here we are."

Kelsey climbed out and stared at the trail cutting through the pines. "Are we going on a picnic?" Her eyes sparkled with life. "The last time I went on one was…"

Jordan waited for the rest of the sentence, wanting to know what Kelsey was about to reveal about her life. When her expectant look was ignored, she popped the trunk, slung the blanket over her shoulder, and lifted the picnic basket out. "As a matter of fact, we are."

She wanted to take Kelsey's hand, but knew it was crossing the line. Instead, she led the way down the path. Birds squawked at the disturbance and flew from nests with a loud flutter of wings. They continued walking until they came to a large clearing with a section of bright green grass. A cutout in the trees formed a perfect circle above them, giving life to the grass.

Jordan spread the blanket and kicked her shoes off. Kelsey followed suit, then dropped to her knees. She rolled over onto her back and stared up through the trees. "Wow. Look at those clouds."

Jordan lay down beside her. "I love this place."

"Do you make a habit of bringing women here?"

Jordan grinned. "I come here to be *alone* and think."

"About what?"

"Anything…everything…nothing in particular."

Kelsey gazed around. "I need a place like this. It's so peaceful and secluded."

Jordan twisted to stare at her. "Yes, very secluded." She wiggled her eyebrows.

Raw desire played across Kelsey's face. She opened

the picnic basket to inspect the contents. "Ooh, strawberries. Yummy."

"And whipped cream," Jordan added.

Kelsey leaned toward her and clamped her mouth over Jordan's, slicking her tongue between Jordan's lips. A soft moan brought to life the sleeping embers between Jordan's legs. Kelsey pushed the basket off her lap and pulled Jordan down on top of her. They kissed deeply, then Jordan flipped Kelsey over and started working with the buttons of her flimsy shirt. When the last button opened, she pushed the folds to the side and yanked Kelsey's bra down. Kelsey worked with the clasp of Jordan's jeans, then freed her shirt. They both worked frantically then, peeling off their clothes.

Butterflies fluttered in Jordan's gut as she took in Kelsey's luscious body, spread out and waiting. What she wouldn't give to be an artist at this moment. To be able to capture Kelsey's radiant beauty, those sapphire eyes full of passion and anticipation. Regaining control, she pulled the strawberries and the canister of whipped cream from the basket.

"Where would you like your strawberries and cream, sexy?"

Kelsey grinned. "In the most *delicate* places."

That was all the invitation Jordan needed. She straddled Kelsey's hips, scooped some whipped cream with her index finger, and placed it on top of Kelsey's nipple. When Kelsey gasped softly, Jordan inserted a strawberry in her mouth.

"Suck this, while I suck other places."

She repeated the process for her other nipple, then scooted down Kelsey's legs and spread the cream over her clit and her already wet opening. Kelsey arched. Jordan could hear her sucking and slurping at the strawberry, kicking up the erotic sounds. As she drew back, Kelsey grabbed her hand and started seductively pulling each finger into her mouth.

Fire crashed between Jordan's legs while her pussy clenched.

She sucked the cream from Kelsey's nipples, taking each deep inside her mouth, running her tongue over the hardened length. Kelsey's teeth clamped on one of Jordan's fingers as a low rumble vibrated inside her chest. Jordan sucked her nipples with just as much hungry need.

Kelsey hissed and wriggled. Releasing Jordan's hand, she dug her fingers through her hair, pushing her head down to force a nipple deeper. "Fuck me, Jordan."

The breathless plea was more than Jordan could bear. She shimmied down the length of Kelsey's body and rammed her fingers inside, filling her completely. Her reward was a passionate squeal. Kelsey ground her hips in demand. Jordan drove harder and faster, stroke after stroke, sucking and licking the cream from Kelsey's clit at the same time. Fingers dug at her hair, this time holding her while Kelsey pumped against her face.

When her orgasm diminished to light pulses, Kelsey sagged back onto the ground and her hands fell limply to the blanket. A loud sigh escaped her as Jordan eased her fingers from their warm, wet haven and kissed a trail to Kelsey's mouth. Kelsey opened her eyes to stare at her, and Jordan felt her insides plummet on a roller coaster. She licked at Kelsey's lips until they parted, inviting her in.

As they kissed, Kelsey rolled her onto her back. Her fingers ran along Jordan's jaw and cheek, coming to rest deep in the strands of her hair.

She finally broke free of Jordan's lips and smiled brightly. "And where would you like your fruit?"

CHAPTER EIGHT

Kelsey knew she had to find a stopping point quickly. The game had continued too long. Yet the more time she spent with Jordan, the more she wondered if she would be different from the others. Jordan made her feel at ease, like she might be more understanding than anyone else. The way she held Kelsey, and listened when she talked, made her think she could open her heart. The idea frightened her. She'd never told a lover how she really felt. Her entire life had been about learning how to disguise her emotions. Showing them made her feel exposed.

Tomorrow she would go back to her normal life of working, dancing, and coming home alone. She'd never look at strawberries again without thinking of Jordan, and she knew she wouldn't find anyone else who could make her feel so completely alive.

Jordan would return to her world, too, and soon they'd be too busy to even think about each other. Kelsey would always remember their time together. She was fooling herself if she tried to believe anything different. She wanted their last night to be unforgettable. It had to be. She needed something to hang on to.

She stared out at the familiar Los Angeles skyline as they drove toward her neighborhood. The sun had laid its head on the horizon as they made love one last time on the blanket. Street lights and stores glistened against a dark sky. Late-night shoppers ambled on the sidewalks carrying bags.

Her heart felt heavy as her gates came into view. Jordan punched in the code, then parked in the circular drive. She turned the motor off immediately, signaling her intentions. Kelsey smiled. She hadn't even considered that Jordan might just drop her off and leave. They were going to spend the night together, and they both knew it. They walked in silence to the front door.

"I'll go get some iced tea," Kelsey said, as if this was just any night. As if they had a routine like couples did, coming home together and settling in to share another evening.

After they'd freshened up, they put on a movie and snuggled on the couch.

"You know, I don't even know your last name." Jordan pressed her lips against Kelsey's cheek.

Kelsey felt all her worries lift. Could she trust Jordan? It gave her a rush of pleasure to think she could bare her soul to someone. She settled back and trailed her fingers over Jordan's taut, muscled stomach through her shirt.

"Kelsey Billings," she said quietly.

"Kelsey Billings. Hmm. Sexy. And familiar."

Kelsey hugged her close and parted her lips, allowing Jordan's tongue to drift inside. Her heart twisted inside her chest. Warmth ignited between her legs. She straddled Jordan's lap and they kissed for a while, tenderly and slowly, then rested their foreheads, one against the other.

"Tell me about yourself," Kelsey asked despite her plan to avoid personal details. "Do you have family?"

Jordan stared at her lips. "You don't want to hear about my screwed-up family."

But she did. She wanted to know everything about Jordan. What made her tick. What her hopes and dreams were. What the hell made her so different.

"Tell me anyway," she insisted.

Jordan's hands slid around Kelsey's waist. "Well, my dad died several years ago and my mom recently lost her job after thirty years. The owner was going bankrupt. Some rich-ass company bought the place and tossed out all of the employees."

Kelsey's vision blurred. Cold chills raced the length of her spine. Jordan's voice sounded far away. What were the odds? She said a silent prayer that some other company was responsible.

"Wow." Jordan gave her a reassuring smile. "Don't look so heartbroken."

Kelsey blinked, and her vision and hearing snapped back to normal. "What?"

"You have the worst look on your face." Jordan dropped a kiss on her cheek. "Don't get upset about it. My mom sure isn't. She thinks the phone will ring any day and someone will want to hire a woman in her fifties who worked all her life in a pharmaceutical lab."

Kelsey gave her a weak smile and tossed names around in her head. Wilson, McGregor, Hominy—all pharmaceutical plants they'd purchased in the last two years. *Dear God, please don't let it be one of them.*

"She had to sell her house," Jordan continued. "And she refused to come live with me. Instead she settled on moving to the projects. It's sad. Our parents aren't supposed to live in poverty, you know? She won't take anything from me. Not even a bag of groceries. It breaks my heart every time I visit her."

"Can't you find another way to help her? Maybe help her get a job?"

Jordan shook her head. "My mom's very independent. She'd die if she knew I've called every pharmaceutical company within a fifty-mile radius. It's her age. No one wants to hire someone who's nearing retirement."

"I'm sorry." Kelsey hugged her.

She suddenly felt spoiled. She'd never lived from paycheck to paycheck. But she'd never been the rotten rich kid who snubbed her nose at people less fortunate, either. Quite the opposite. When it came to the underdog, she was right there to lend a helping hand. Then again, no one would know how much she donated to charities or what she tried to do to build a better world. Ripping apart struggling businesses was her job, and for a long time she'd accepted her father's rationalizations.

According to John Billings, people who lost their jobs were absorbed back into the workplace. They retrained. They took advantage of new opportunities. Some had always dreamed of their own small businesses and being laid off finally gave them the chance to make it on their own. Those who didn't…well, wasn't survival of the fittest nature's plan for all species?

"I'm sure she'll find something soon." Kelsey slid off Jordan's lap onto the couch. She said a silent prayer before she asked the next question. "What did your mother do at her plant?" She was terrified to hear the answer.

"She was the owner's bookkeeper. She had a few years of chemical experience, but nothing that would look good on her resume."

The question was on the tip of Kelsey's tongue. She fought against asking, but lost the battle. "What was the name of the company she worked for?"

"McGregor Pharmaceuticals."

Sickness rolled through Kelsey's stomach. She'd never imagined wanting to flee from Jordan, but right now she wanted to be anywhere but here. She blankly stared at the TV screen, her insides coiled in a knot.

Jordan pulled her close. "That's really the whole story. I don't have brothers or sisters. It's just me and Mom." On a bitter note, she added. "I wish she'd let me take care of her."

Tears welled in Kelsey's eyes at the distress in Jordan's voice. How would she feel if she knew the truth? Kelsey didn't have a clue what to say or do. If she spoke out, Jordan would leave. What would that accomplish? Nothing could change what had happened, so why destroy their last few hours together? Now that she knew about Jordan's mom, it didn't seem right to say nothing. But she wanted them to have one more night. Was she only thinking of her own needs? And Lord, how she needed Jordan between her thighs.

Tomorrow this would all be over. But tonight, Jordan was all hers. She'd be damned if she wasted another second talking about anything else.

Jordan must have noticed her change of mood. "I didn't mean to upset you. I know you have problems of your own. That woman at the bar scared the shit out of me." Her grin formed against Kelsey's cheek. "And I don't scare very easily."

Kelsey gave a small, guilty nod. She eased off the couch and pulled Jordan up. Silently, she led her to the bedroom. She wanted to feel her quiver one more time, wanted to hear her soft cries of pleasure. *Just one more fucking time*. She pushed her onto the bed. With trembling fingers, she undressed while Jordan discarded her own shirt and jeans.

When their last garments landed in a heap on the floor, Kelsey crept onto the bed and knelt next to Jordan. Turning toward her, Jordan tenderly palmed her ass, squeezing her cheeks. Her emerald eyes were warm with desire, but another emotion lingered in their depths. Wanting to erase the sadness she could see, Kelsey cupped her face and kissed her slowly and passionately. Their mouths explored and consumed. Soft moans blended with damp breaths as they surfaced to stare at each other.

Kelsey pushed Jordan flat on her back. She wanted to touch, taste, and lick every part of her. She slithered down her body and ran her tongue along Jordan's leg, taking a quick nip above her kneecap. Jordan chuckled and opened her legs. Kelsey continued her way to Jordan's crotch. Hungrily she sucked at her clit and drove her fingers inside.

Jordan arched and let out a deep groan, grinding her hips. She looked so free and beautiful in her arousal, a lump rose in Kelsey's throat. She squeezed her eyes shut to block out the image. If only she could unleash her burdens. How wonderful it would feel to bare her soul for a change, instead of hiding her dirty little secrets. Sometimes she seemed doomed to carry the unbearable weight of her father's past as well as her own. She was tired and just wanted everything to stop.

"Is something wrong?" Jordan asked, and Kelsey realized she was completely still. Her head was resting on Jordan's belly and her fingers were loosely buried.

She looked up and managed a sexy smile. "Just making you wait."

Turn off your thoughts. There was nothing she could do. This was her destiny and tonight was the last time she was ever going to be with this woman.

Jordan smiled back at her. "Whatever I did, tell me, so I can do it again."

Kelsey plunged her fingers faster until Jordan screamed, body writhing. When she stopped quivering, Kelsey moved from between her legs and climbed up her body. She studied Jordan, memorizing every contour, and then continued her climb until she straddled her face. Jordan tongued her clit. Her hands cupped Kelsey's ass cheeks, holding her in place. She lapped at her pussy with her long, pleasing tongue, and then eagerly sucked her clit. Kelsey whipped her head back and pumped her hips, catching the rhythm of her sucking.

Jordan's fingers slipped between Kelsey's legs. She rammed them inside.

Kelsey screamed, "Harder." Her insides coiled like a spring.

With speed she could have only learned over many years of karate, Jordan grabbed her waist and flipped her on her back. Kelsey bounced on the mattress while Jordan rolled on top of her.

"Where are your toys?" Jordan shoved her legs apart and pushed her fingers back inside.

Kelsey jerked her hips and dug her fingers into the comforter. "I don't need toys. Just…you."

A confused expression slipped across Jordan's face.

Something had gone wrong. Kelsey could feel it deep in her heart. Their last night would be nothing but a good-bye fuck. Instead of making love, they would keep a safe distance and escape, as they always did, into physical intensity. She should want a hard fuck, shouldn't she? As if that would make her feel better about the lies she hid from Jordan. Turmoil twisted in her head.

Jordan's brow creased. "What's wrong?"

Tears welled. Kelsey took a deep breath, willing the tears to disappear. "Nothing. I want you to finish what you started." She smiled weakly and arched her hips.

Jordan leaned back and opened the drawer to the nightstand. Kelsey caught sight of the strap-on and tensed. She didn't want their last night to be spent with fakeness, but she willed desire onto her face. If Jordan wanted this, she sure as hell would be an accepting recipient. She wanted Jordan to remember their last night together for the rest of her life.

Watching Kelsey's face closely, Jordan hesitated, the strap-on dangling from her hand. She could see that something was wrong. She'd been feeling it in the way Kelsey was acting. She had no idea what had happened, but she wasn't going to play the game with her. She didn't want to start asking questions and turn their last night into a therapy session. She'd come here to give Kelsey the best fuck she'd ever had. Afterward, she would snuggle up beside her and hold her until she fell asleep. No analysis. No excuses. No awkward conversation as they tried to say good-bye. When Kelsey woke up in the morning, Jordan would be gone.

She pulled the straps around her legs and snapped the rivets. When she looked down at Kelsey, the passion on her face tied her stomach in a knot. Her expression demanded: *Get that fucking thing in me right now.* Jordan grabbed the head of the dildo and leaned between Kelsey's legs.

"Stop stalling and do it," Kelsey said, but there was something strange about her tone. Her face might say *fuck me*, but her voice didn't.

Jordan wanted to yank the device and trash the damn thing. She started to lean back, but Kelsey wrapped her legs around her hips and locked her in place.

"Fuck me, Jordan."

Jordan slowly guided the dildo inside, sliding easily into her wet pussy. Kelsey cried out and arched, digging her fingers into Jordan's back.

"Oh, yes. Harder!" She pumped steadily beneath her. "Faster, Jordan."

Jordan leaned back on her heels. Kelsey unlocked the vise grip around her back. Jordan paced herself and slid in and out, thumbing Kelsey's clit in steady circles. Kelsey pumped and arched, catching her strokes, releasing soft cries as she climbed closer to the edge.

"You can't do any better than that?"

Jordan rammed harder. "You said you wanted a fuck, not a banging."

Kelsey threw her head back. "Oh God, that's more like it. Don't stop."

Jordan shoved one of Kelsey's legs toward her chest. Kelsey grabbed hold and held tight, opening herself for deeper penetration. Jordan pounded against her, making their sweaty bodies bounce. She rammed home hard, working Kelsey's clit with perfect rhythm.

Kelsey gasped for breath and released a loud, piercing scream. Her body rocked wildly. Jordan let loose of her legs and fell down on top of her, grinding her hips. When she sought Kelsey's lips, Kelsey turned her head and sank her fingers into Jordan's hair. She yanked and pulled, still thrashing wildly against her, until the orgasm ran its course.

"That was awesome," she gasped out as Jordan kissed her neck.

Jordan smiled but couldn't reply. She wasn't sure which part was awesome, the orgasm or the good-bye fuck. She was sure this was Kelsey's way of saying *adiós*. Time to get back to the real world.

She eased the dildo out, tore it from her body, and tossed it to the floor. When she turned back, Kelsey was already on her side. Jordan spooned in behind her and wrapped her arms around her. She bunched the soft cotton sheet around their sweat-sticky bodies and waited. This was the moment when one of them should say something about the future, but Jordan wasn't willing to go out on a limb. Not when Kelsey had already shown her the door. She didn't seem open to any kind of discussion, and even if she had been considering the possibilities, she'd probably made her choice after hearing about Jordan's mom. Who would want to get involved with a woman whose mother would soon be a dependant?

Jordan frowned. That wasn't the reason. She'd seen compassion in Kelsey. Her strained look when they were talking wasn't phony. She was genuinely upset to hear about Susan Porter's plight. Maybe her reaction was just sympathy for Jordan, but it was almost like she felt a sense of responsibility. How odd, and how adorably sweet.

Fuck. She had to stop thinking about her. It was over. But God, how Kelsey burned in her mind. Forgetting about her was going to be tough. She felt Kelsey's shoulders sag and watched her chest rise and fall with deep, steady breaths. Kissing her cheek, Jordan released a resigned sigh and slid out of bed.

After she'd donned her clothes, she stood staring at Kelsey's beautiful face and body. There were so many things she wanted to say, but her time with Kelsey was over.

It was time to go.

CHAPTER NINE

After a long week, Kelsey sank into the chair at her dressing table and stared at her reflection. Her spirits should be lifted, here in her home away from home, yet this blue funk had a death grip on her. She checked her makeup and wondered if Jordan would show up tonight. Her heart flipped at the thought, but she knew better. Jordan hadn't set foot in The Pink Lady since their good-bye fuck, and Kelsey didn't expect anything different. They both knew the score. The fling was over. They weren't going to become friends or anything. Jordan was a good fuck, and that was that.

Pushing out of the chair, Kelsey smoothed her thin miniskirt, donned the mask, and walked down the hall. She kept her eyes glued to the floor when Max screamed her name. She didn't want to see the ogling women waiting for her. Once she made it through the curtains to the stool, she eased over on her stomach and spread her legs open.

Whistles pierced the air. Thundering music pounded in her ears. The wall of sound shut out her thoughts and she became herself under the blaring speakers. Devoid of feelings. Calm and in control. While cheers echoed off the walls and stomping feet shook the floorboards, she cat-pranced across the stage, allowing hands to feel her arms and legs. A few brave souls grasped at strands of her long, flowing hair. Kelsey swept past them disdainfully.

She grabbed a hand protruding in the air and licked the tips of a few fingers. Images of Jordan found their way inside her head where nothing but the music and shouting was allowed. Fire crashed between her thighs at the memory of Jordan's fingers ramming deep inside. She shoved the woman's hand between her legs and ground her hips against the knuckles. But she couldn't block out Jordan's touch.

Her crotch soaked automatically. She ground harder until fleshy, unfamiliar fingers wandered beneath her thong. Kelsey looked directly into a pair of chestnut brown eyes. A grin spread across the woman's face. She attempted to slide her fingers deeper inside Kelsey's thong. Kelsey tossed the groping hand away and rose above the crowd.

Oh, yeah. This was where she belonged. This was where the world outside shimmered away, where her real life paled in comparison. She strutted across the stage, passing more faces, more smiles. She had a hell of a lot of drooling fans.

The music ended too soon. She didn't want the sound to cease and the silence to drag her back to reality. She left the stage and ran to her dressing room. Halfway down the hall, she removed the mask and halter top, not caring who saw her. She threw both against the wall as soon as she entered her dressing room. The miniskirt hit the floor. She kicked off her heels and grabbed a pair of jeans. A sleeveless T-shirt soon covered her naked breasts. A sound caught her attention, and she spun to find Sharon standing in the doorway.

"You okay?" Sharon kept her distance. "You're not yourself tonight."

Kelsey nodded. "A-okay, boss."

"Wanna talk about it?"

Kelsey didn't know what was wrong with her. Where the

hell was her strong-woman persona vanishing to? "Really. I'm fine, Sharon. Don't worry."

"Kelsey, I can't help if you're not honest with me. I think it's time to call Artie." Sharon approached and held out an envelope. "You got another letter."

Kelsey took it with caution, her stomach knotting into a cramp. She slowly tore off the end, extracted the folded note, and read the latest threat. It was neatly typed, like the first one.

AN EYE FOR AN EYE. A TOOTH FOR A TOOTH.
YOUR DEATH FOR ANOTHER.

"You can't handle this on your own," Sharon said. "What if it's not just a joke? What if Paula's out for revenge?"

Kelsey shook her head. "I don't want to overreact." Her hands shook. She hid them between her knees.

"She was virtually foaming at the mouth in here the other night."

"She was drunk," Kelsey said. "And she didn't admit she wrote that note or made the calls. Besides, the Riching takeover was one of the easiest I ever helped Dad with. Her father never fought the sale. I think he was glad it was over."

Sharon sighed. "I'm sorry about that night. I guess I was a little jealous."

Kelsey smiled at her abrupt change of subject. "Don't sweat it."

Even though Sharon had only been blowing off steam and they were still friends, Kelsey didn't want her knowing too much. She wasn't willing to talk about Jordan. If Sharon knew, she would think the end of the fling had something to do with her, God forbid.

"Have you told her about your company?" Sharon probed.

"Told who?"

"Don't act like you don't know who I'm talking about."

Kelsey shrugged. "There's no need to tell her. You know me. When it's just sex, what else is there to discuss?"

"Are you sure?" Sharon sounded suspicious. Her eyes combed Kelsey's face.

"Hell yes, I'm sure." Kelsey laughed. "I don't have time for mushy love shit. Besides, you're the only person who doesn't care about my real job. Then again, you're a bitch, so you don't count."

Sharon chuckled. "Yep. I'm one of a kind, all right." She started back toward the doorway. "But sooner or later you have to trust someone."

"I trust the people who love me," Kelsey said.

Sharon gave her a long look. "That's why you need to trust me, and call Artie."

Nodding, Kelsey slid the note back into the envelope.

Darren rushed in before she could escape. "Wanna go grab a bite to eat with me and Tony after we lock up?"

"You bet." Kelsey dropped the death threat into the top drawer of her dressing table.

Sharon gave her a questioning look. "I could call Artie, if you like."

"No." Kelsey stood. "This is my problem, not yours."

Darren cocked an eyebrow. "Are you keeping secrets from me?"

"Would Kelsey do that to her friends?" Sharon said sarcastically.

As she stalked away, Darren planted a hand on his hip. "Kelsey, honey, did it ever occur to you that you don't have to defend yourself from *everyone*?"

Kelsey remained quiet, but his words jolted something loose in her heart. Was that what she did? She stared at her face in the mirror, drawn back in time to another time and another face. The reflection of her mother bounced from her memory to the glass surface in front of her. Like watching an old movie, Kelsey saw her crying. She tried to comfort her, placing an arm around her shoulders.

Her mother heaved a huge sigh. "Nothing will ever change. He even thinks he has to protect himself against me."

The defeat in her face made Kelsey feel just as helpless as she had all those years ago. Her mother had given up. She had stopped loving him. Kelsey had always seen *her* as the traitor, the one who walked away and started a new life. But was the betrayal completely one-sided? For the first time in her life she understood that her father had caused pain to the woman who loved him and that there were consequences. He had paid a price for putting a wall between himself and the people who truly cared about him.

Did she want to make the same mistake?

❖

Jordan pulled into the parking lot of the all-night restaurant and checked the time. Connie probably wouldn't arrive for another ten minutes. Jordan was early because she desperately needed her old friend right now and because she didn't want to park down the road near The Pink Lady. She was going crazy at home and had to find something to wipe away the damn images coursing her mind. TV wasn't helping. She couldn't sleep, either. And without decent rest, she couldn't function, let alone train for the upcoming match. At this rate she would be publicly humiliated by a lesser opponent.

Why couldn't she stop thinking about Kelsey?

And then there was her mother, acting so calm during her visit. The woman was truly going to give Jordan an ulcer. Her savings were draining at a fast clip, and there wasn't a damn thing Jordan could do about it. She ground her teeth in irritation. Over the past week, she'd tried calling pharmaceutical plants in other states, as well as drugstores, and still hadn't found anything.

She felt hopeless and scared. Her mother seemed to be in

denial about her shrinking options, still stubbornly insisting that she had things under control and could manage on her own. What was it going to take to make her accept the situation and allow Jordan to do what any daughter would want to do?

She locked the Viper and strode into the diner expecting to have to wait alone. But she heard her name called and spotted a redhead waving from a window booth. Just seeing Connie's smile put Jordan at ease. God, how she needed to release some of this pent-up frustration. If anyone could get her back on track, it was her old college roommate.

"You haven't called me in, like, months," Connie complained as Jordan slid into the booth to sit next to her.

"I'm sorry." Jordan hung her head in an attempt to make Connie feel sorry for her.

"You should be." Connie grinned. "Your mom find a job?"

Jordan shook her head. "She's still looking, and she still won't let me help her."

"That's because she's a classy broad. She's not gonna mooch off her daughter."

Jordan shrugged and leaned back. "I guess. She won't have a choice when her savings bleed dry."

"Then you'll deal with it when that happens."

They ordered a couple of beers and studied the menu.

"The blue cheese burger is good," Jordan said. She usually came here before heading to one of the clubs in the next block.

"Want to share an appetizer?" Connie asked. "I'm starving."

Jordan had no appetite. She'd been living off fruit and coffee for days. To make Connie happy she said, "Sure. Whatever you feel like."

"Onion rings." Connie dropped the menu. "And maybe a malt. Chocolate or vanilla?"

Jordan's stomach churned. "You choose."

The waitress poured their beer into glasses at the table and took their meal order.

"Now, onto the good stuff," Connie said as soon as she walked away. "Your sex life."

Jordan smiled. Leave it to Connie to jump right to the smut of the matter, and to know there was a woman in the mix. "It's not worth talking about. Not anymore."

Connie studied her face. "Since when? That bitch Marsha didn't ruin your libido, did she? I told you not to let her move in."

Jordan laughed. "No. I just, well…" She took a deep breath. If she couldn't tell Connie her feelings, who the hell could she tell? "I met someone. A stripper."

"Oh, do tell." Connie cozied against the booth.

"It's nothing. I just—"

"Fucked her? Tell *that* part."

Jordan grinned and sipped her beer thoughtfully. "I don't know. It was different."

Connie angled her head. "Different? You better explain that one, 'cause for a second there I thought I saw Cupids and puppies floating across your eyes."

Jordan glanced back across her shoulder as the glass door swung open and several people made a noisy entrance. A feminine laugh and male giggles filled the diner. Jordan's breath caught at the sight of Kelsey with Darren and another man. Her long hair spiraled over her shoulders in a cascade of pale honey curls. The bright overhead lights drained the color from her cheeks and made the contours of her face seem sharper than usual. She looked between Jordan and Connie, and quickly glanced away. The unmistakable jealousy in her expression, not to mention the jeans that dipped dangerously low on her hips, made heat curl between Jordan's thighs.

Darren's smile slid from his face when he saw Connie. He

turned a death glare on Jordan, letting her know in no uncertain terms that he'd rather bitch slap her than witness her sharing dinner with another woman. Obviously Kelsey hadn't mentioned that their affair was history.

Connie shifted beside her. "What's up?"

Jordan looked away from the fire dancing in Kelsey's eyes. "That's *her*."

Connie twisted in her seat. "Ooh-la-la. She looks pissed."

Pissed *and* jealous. Jordan grinned. She could work with this. She smiled as the trio moved toward them.

"Hi. You guys just get off?" She lost her battle not to look at Kelsey.

Darren giggled. "We haven't gotten *off*...yet." He blew a kiss at the man standing next to him. "This gorgeous hunk is Tony."

Jordan smiled at their display of affection and ached that she couldn't have something so natural and easy with Kelsey. "Nice to meet you, Tony. Want to join us?"

Kelsey's eyes shot cold blue sparks at her. "No, thank you. I wouldn't want to interrupt your date."

"I do. Sit." Darren shoved Tony ahead of him into the booth.

Jordan fought back the urge to laugh out loud. Kelsey was so fucking jealous. "We don't mind." She elbowed Connie. "Do we?"

Connie played along. "No, not at all."

Kelsey pulled a chair up to the end of the table, keeping distance between them, her eyes trained on the windows.

"We've ordered, but I'll get the waitress," Jordan offered helpfully.

"Oh, don't bother," Darren said. "We're regulars. They know what we want." His eyes moved over Connie again. He brushed some imaginary fluff off his shoulder.

Kelsey drummed her fingernails on the table, looking anywhere but at Jordan. Fury oozed from her.

Jordan said the first thing that popped into her mind. "So, nice hot weather coming tomorrow, huh?"

She did not just say that. *Please God, let me sink into the La Brea Tar Pits right this minute.* Wasn't she supposed to be working Kelsey's jealousy?

Connie snickered. "My little weather girl." She patted Jordan's leg.

Kelsey turned an icy stare on her.

Darren coughed. He informed Connie, "Kelsey's a black belt."

Connie smiled. "Me, too. Jordan trained me. Private lessons, naturally."

Jordan took a sip of beer to keep from doubling over with laughter. The fire and ice mingling in Kelsey's eyes was too much.

"Well, Kelsey has a *stalker*." Darren sounded like a petulant second grader, daring Connie to one-up him.

Connie scooted closer, faking seduction. "Jordan would never allow anyone to stalk me. Would you, baby?"

Jordan swallowed a laugh and slowly shook her head. "Never."

Their food arrived. Tony ate like he wished he wasn't sitting there. Darren squirted ketchup over Connie's food "by accident." Jordan nibbled on a buffalo wing and couldn't keep her eyes off Kelsey. Her mind stretched as she tried to find something to say. *You look so hot I want to make you come. Guess what, I missed you.* She stuffed a fry into her mouth to stifle the groan.

"How long have you two known each other?" Kelsey's voice was neurotic.

Before Jordan could put her foot in her mouth and end the glorious pleasure of teasing her, Connie snickered. Turning to Jordan, she said, "Oh, what, like twenty years now?"

Kelsey's eyes widened. "Twenty years?"

Darren huffed. "Why, you two-timing tramp." He shuffled out of the booth and yanked Tony with him. "Come on, Kelsey, honey. You need a good delousing. Miss Thing may have given you cooties."

He continued tossing insults over his shoulder as he pranced toward the cashier.

Kelsey took several steps toward the door, then swung around, her face contorted in a mask of rage. She prowled back to the table. "You're a sleazebag. How dare you?"

"Holy shit." Connie gave a low whistle after the doors swung closed behind the trio. "That's one fireball you've got on your hands."

Jordan stared out the window, watching Kelsey stomp across the parking lot followed by Darren and his date.

"Why are you still sitting here, you idiot?" Connie said. "Go stop her."

"What the fuck for? She just dumped me."

Connie pushed her out of the booth. "Get your ass out there before she leaves. I think Cupid has found his target."

❖

Kelsey stopped by Darren's car and waited for the lovebirds. Anger rumbled, and her temper spiked. Jesus, she'd never been so jealous in her life, and for what? A two-timer who had cheated on her girlfriend. God, she felt dirty and humiliated.

Darren and Tony giggled as they ambled toward her.

"Will you two stop groping each other long enough to take me back to the club? I knew I should have driven my own car."

"Never mind, guys. I'll take her. It's on my way." Jordan stepped off the curb.

Kelsey turned a furious glare her way. "No way. You don't get to cheat on your girlfriend with me, again." She scowled at Darren, urging him to hurry. "Get in the damn car."

Darren gave Jordan an appraising look. "Maybe you should go with her, honey," he told Kelsey. Smiling up at his date, he added, "My little cupcake is feeling neglected. Aren't you, cupcake?"

Furious, Kelsey gritted her teeth and practically growled at Jordan. "I'll walk."

Jordan forked her fingers through her hair in a gesture of frustration. "You're being stalked, goddammit. You're not walking anywhere."

Kelsey turned and started to march off, but Jordan grabbed her and spun her around. "Get in the fucking car or I'll put you there myself."

Kelsey gave an impressive display of the haughty princess, squaring her shoulders, lifting her chin, and sweeping past Jordan to the passenger side of the Viper. She stood there, forcing Jordan to open the door for her. Without a word, she settled into the seat and snapped the seat belt in place.

The two-block drive proved more uncomfortable than a meeting between the Palestinians and the Israelis. Neither of them wanted to be the first to speak. Unable to hold back her anger, Kelsey twisted to face Jordan as soon as they reached The Pink Lady.

"You've got some nerve. Were you fucking me while your little girlfriend sat at home and worried?"

Jordan grinned. She looked positively ecstatic at the furious accusation. "No. I was fucking you while she worked."

Kelsey gasped. She balled her fists and stilled the impulse to swing. "You're sick."

"You didn't seem to mind while you were screaming my name."

Kelsey's pussy tightened. God, how could Jordan still make her want to rip off her clothes? *Dear Lord, I was the other woman.* And loved every second of it. Terrified that Jordan would see the need in her eyes, she stared out the window. Tears stung her lids but she willed them back. She'd be damned if this bitch made her cry, no matter how hurt she was.

"Kelsey, look at me."

Jordan's plea was like a path of fire to her gut. Desire and longing speared her pussy like shards of hot glass. "Fuck you."

Jordan tucked her finger under Kelsey's chin and coaxed her head around. "Connie's my best friend. We were college roommates."

Kelsey swallowed. Those eyes, soft with amusement and honesty, made her want to straddle Jordan's face. *Twenty years.* The comment finally made sense. She had assumed they were childhood sweethearts, which made Jordan's behavior seem even more callous. God, she'd just acted like a love-struck fool, and in public. She'd been played.

Jordan's delicate smile and soft, teasing expression did nothing to appease her. Suddenly she felt like a scorned lover. Embarrassment set in, renewing her anger. She turned away, afraid of the look on Jordan's face, and afraid of the emotions churning in her stomach like a building tsunami.

Pressing her cheek to the cool glass window, she said, "Very funny."

"I'm not the one leading a double life." Jordan's tone was serious. "I don't even know who you really are, Kelsey."

"What do you mean?"

"I've been to your house. And I saw you in your business suit one day. Obviously you're not stripping to put food on the table."

Kelsey faced her once more. Her mouth trembled. She wanted to spill out everything, but she didn't know where to begin. "You know me better than you think."

"Really? Because we fucked a few times?"

"No." Kelsey struggled for the right words. Tears refused her efforts to blink them back. "The picnic. It was one of the happiest days of my life."

What was she trying to say? That it was the only day in recent memory that she'd felt *real.* That when she and Jordan made love on that blanket, she'd felt *loved.*

Jordan stared at her for a long time. "I'm going to drive you home, and then we're going to talk."

Kelsey's pulse stampeded. Was this a mistake? Ignoring her doubts, she said, "Okay."

"And I want the truth," Jordan said.

"I know."

Kelsey let her head sink back against the leather seat, shocked by the risk she was about to take. Jordan wanted the truth and she would get it. Every last dirty fact. It would be a huge relief to let go of all that she kept secret. No matter what happened.

Chapter Ten

Kelsey's gate was wide open. Toilet paper was strewn over the bushes and trees like Christmas decorations. Red paint splattered the front of the house in a cruel attempt to ruin its beauty.

"Oh, my God." Kelsey jumped from the Viper as soon they parked.

Jordan pulled her cell phone from her pocket and dialed 911. She got out of the car and walked close on Kelsey's heels, searching the yard.

The operator answered, "911. What's your emergency?"

"Someone broke into my friend's house. We need an officer here immediately." Jordan gave the address.

"Ma'am, is anyone there with you?"

"My friend is here. She owns the house."

The dispatcher told her to stay on the phone until the police arrived, and Jordan put her arm around Kelsey. "They're on their way."

"What kind of sick fuck would do this?" Tears streamed down Kelsey's beautiful face as she looked out over the lawn.

Probably the same sick fuck who sent death threats to the club. Jordan kept that thought to herself. The woman Harold had wrestled to the floor hadn't denied making the threats, and everyone seemed to think she could be responsible. Had she been out here to Kelsey's home? And if she knew where Kelsey lived, what else did she know? How were she and Kelsey connected?

Jordan walked with Kelsey to survey the damage. Broken glass littered the tropical undergrowth along the edge of the driveway. Upon further inspection, they found a few busted windows and more toilet paper thrown from inside the house. Kelsey stepped up to the wooden porch.

"Don't go inside." Jordan stalled her. "Wait for the police to get here."

Kelsey gave a piercing shriek and covered her mouth with her hands. Following the direction of her horrified gaze, Jordan felt a chill. The muscles in her back contracted. Deep, swirling scratches covered the patio boards in front of the door, spelling out a new threat.

TIME TO DIE BITCH

Kelsey's shaking sobs wrenched Jordan's heart. She held her close as the police approached with lights flashing and sirens blaring as if they'd spotted a terrorist. Their swift arrival amazed her, but she supposed one of the advantages of a neighborhood like this one was that the cops came when they were called. If she'd dialed 911 from her mother's apartment, the response time would have been very different, if they bothered to show up at all. She nudged the bitter feeling away when Kelsey moved out of her arms.

They both faced the bright lights.

After confirming with the dispatcher that the police were now present, Jordan ended the call and led Kelsey away from the porch. If the stalker had left any evidence, she didn't want to trample it before the police could take a look.

A tall officer in plain clothes approached them and shined a flashlight against the backdrop of the house. "Has anyone been inside?"

"No." Kelsey wiped the tears from her face.

The officer gave some orders and dug in his pocket. Handing a uniformed officer a key, he said, "Go make sure the house is clear." He turned back to them. "Do you know who might have done this, Kelsey?"

Acting like it was nothing to hear this police commander using her first name, Kelsey said, "I guess we could go down the list."

To Jordan's astonishment, he responded by drawing Kelsey into his muscular arms. "It's okay, baby doll. There's an old saying: Keep your friends close and your enemies closer. Your daddy lived by that rule."

"Oh, Artie," Kelsey sighed. "I should have called you sooner."

Artie? First-name basis with police officers? Who the hell was this woman?

Artie patted her back and then released her. "It sounds like there's a lot we need to talk about."

"That's an understatement." Kelsey gave a shy grin to Jordan. "Jordan, meet my second dad, Artie Whitaker. My father's best friend."

Artie stuck out his wide hand, and Jordan shook it. She wanted to scream questions at the both of them, but keeping quiet seemed best for the time being.

"Nothing inside, Chief," the uniformed officer yelled from the front door. "It's all clear. There's one hell of a mess in here, though."

Kelsey walked in his direction. Jordan followed close behind. Artie Whitaker stayed back and talked into his radio.

More toilet paper and paint bombs littered the rooms behind the shattered windows. Ripped curtains billowed out. Kelsey covered her mouth as they entered a formal living room. Paint balls had shattered a figurine case. Pieces of splintered glass littered the carpet.

"That was my mom's." Tears fell harder down Kelsey's mascara-smeared face. She knelt on the floor lifting pieces of porcelain. A tiara with a gemstone dangling from the center lay twisted against the case. Kelsey reached for it, sobs shaking her body. She clutched it against her chest. "She loved this more than anything."

Artie's voice from the next room tore Jordan's gaze from the pitiful sight. "There's no sign of a forced entry, so I think it's safe to say whoever did this already knew the code."

He came through the doorway, pausing when he saw Kelsey on the floor.

"I want you to fry whoever did it," Kelsey mumbled.

"We will, baby." He stepped around the broken glass and peered through the shattered window. "You can't stay here. You better come stay with me and Ellie. She's been complaining that you never visit us."

"It's okay, sir. She can stay with me," Jordan said. "We have some things to discuss."

Artie nodded. "Good. I'll let you pack a few things, but don't try to clean anything up."

"But I can't just leave it like…this." Kelsey stared down at the mementos.

He crossed the room and touched her shoulder, explaining gently, "We'll have to process the entire house for our investigation. You won't be able to come back until the crime scene unit finishes dusting for fingerprints and checking for evidence."

Jordan took Kelsey's hand. "Come on. Let's go get some clothes for you."

❖

Whoever was toying with her wanted her to live in fear. The monster was winning. She'd never been so scared. She'd had her share of hate mail along with numerous phone calls to the office at Billings Industries. People screamed obscenities and then hung up, as if that put them in control. Paula Riching was the first person to track her down to The Pink Lady, and she was probably the person who had typed the recent notes and made the calls Sharon intercepted. But this? Kelsey had never experienced anything so vengeful. Or so personal. Whoever did this wanted to prove a point, but what that point was, she didn't know.

She returned her concentration to the overnight bag she was packing. Jordan sat on the bed a few feet away, her arms folded. Kelsey hardly dared to look at her hard expression. She was in for a long night of explaining. Was she ready to spill her guts? She was no longer sure if she could bring herself to share her dirty secrets with the woman she'd come to care for and admire. All she wanted to do was curl up on a couch, fall asleep in Jordan's arms, and leave the world and her worries behind.

She still had a choice. She could go to Artie's, where she was safe. He and Ellie knew all there was to know about her and her father, and they didn't judge her.

"Are you ready?" Jordan asked.

Kelsey realized she was staring into space. She straightened and decided it was time to get the confrontation over with. She would just have to put the ball in Jordan's court and see what happened.

Artie was waiting for them on the front lawn. "I need the name and phone numbers of all the people who have the code."

Kelsey felt a jolt in her chest. He'd be proud of her. "I've only given the code to people I trust."

"Good. And why else would you give anyone your code, honey?" He gave her a bright smile, his eyes sparkling with humor. The wind blew his silver hair across his head. "So, how many people have you trusted?"

She gave him an exasperated glare, then started naming. "Darren and Sharon. Kevin. You. Jordan. No one else."

He looked relieved. "That's all?"

Guilt washed over her. There was so much she needed to tell him. "I have a stalker," she blurted before she could change her mind.

His sympathy vanished, replaced by a look of anger. "What do you mean?"

"Someone's been leaving death threats at the club. Notes. Phone calls. A woman showed up the other night, called me every name in the book, and then made some threats before Harold tossed her out. He got her name and tag."

Artie flipped open a new page in his notebook. "As much as you'd like to play tough girl, there are some things you can't handle alone. What's her name?"

"Paula Riching." Kelsey watched Artie's gaze go from a hardened stare to a confused glare. Dreading to tell him the next part, she dragged in a long breath. "We bought her dad's company."

His gaze flew up. "Why didn't you tell me any of this before?"

There it was, the protectiveness that made her feel secure. He'd stepped in and never missed a beat from where her father left off. She adored him for loving her so much.

"I didn't want to worry you." She looked into his eyes. "And I thought she was just venting."

Artie scribbled something down on the pad. "Go get some sleep and let me take care of this. But you better call me first thing in the morning. We have a few things to discuss."

Kelsey knew he wouldn't say too much in front of Jordan, and she wanted to hug him for his discretion. She glanced at Jordan and caught a look that told her they would be getting to the bottom of her mysterious life tonight. She wasn't sure why it was so important to bare it all to Jordan, but she wanted to tell her everything. She didn't want any secrets between them. No matter how this night ended, she would tell the truth and have a clear heart and mind.

❖

Jordan steered the Viper down a long driveway that wound through a tropical garden. Swaying palm trees stood tall among smaller fan palms, their leaves rustling in the light breeze. The drive ended in front of a large gray stucco house. A porch wrapped around the front and disappeared along both sides. Unlike a lot of houses on the L.A. coastline, this one had a high chimneystack.

Kelsey felt at home at first glance. She couldn't wait to get inside and light the fireplace. Jordan grabbed the overnight bag from behind her seat and Kelsey followed her indoors, through a wide hallway to a grand room with a brown plush couch in the center. A matching love seat and recliner stood on either side, creating a square in the middle of the floor. A glass coffee table added to the comfort.

Kelsey stilled her beating heart at the sight of the rock fireplace. Brass-handled pokers sat on the edge of the hearth. She couldn't wait to light that fire and cuddle up with Jordan.

"Welcome to my humble abode." Jordan tossed her bag on the floor and turned on a lamp in one corner.

Kelsey walked further into the room, looking at all the knickknacks, trophies, medallions, and pictures. Smiling faces filled the space in each frame. Kelsey's heart raced for her father and even for her mooching, non-caring brother. But most especially, she thought about her mother. She missed her something fierce right now. The Billings home used to display the same loving faces before her mom left, and before a heart attack took the life of her father. After that, everything else was downhill until she met Sharon.

Even though she was never in love with her, they'd shared some of the same dreams. With Sharon owning the bar and needing help to bring it to life, Kelsey had jumped right in, exploring her desire to dance. At first she'd planned to strip only a couple of nights a week and strictly on a temporary basis. But dancing carried her away from real life and the business that cost her so much happiness.

Her father's dreams had kept her trudging along day after day, ignoring everything that really mattered in life so she could continue his legacy. If it wasn't for The Pink Lady and her wacky friends, she would have gone insane a long time ago. The bar became a place for her to get away from her burdens, and when the business began to thrive, Kelsey felt proud of her contribution.

Jordan stepped around her. "Would you like me to start a fire, since you can't tear your gaze away from the fireplace?"

At Kelsey's nod, she ignited twigs and loose paper, then sat back to watch the fire roar to life. The muscles jerked in her arms with every log she tossed on the blaze. Kelsey's fantasies were yanked from her mind when Jordan dusted off her hands and flopped down on the couch. *Here we go.*

"You ready to start telling me what the hell's going on?"

"What do you want to know?" Kelsey knew her reply sounded like procrastination. She wasn't trying to play games, she just didn't know where to start.

Jordan eyed her impatiently. "That's a stupid question. I can't remember a cop in the world that ever slid to a scene as fast as those guys did tonight, obviously because you're the chief's daughter-substitute. You strip when you don't need the money. You live in a mansion. And the police seem to be your personal bodyguards." She gave a sarcastic laugh. "That probably rules out drug dealing, but I don't know how you really make your living, and the death threats and vandalism have got me wondering. So what's your story, Kelsey?"

Taking a deep breath, Kelsey stepped around Jordan's legs and sat beside her. "As you know, I don't strip. I'm not that cheap. I dance."

Jordan chuckled. "Okay, I'll give you that one."

"And I told you, I run my father's business. He died almost two years ago. My brother is too stupid to run anything except the engine in his Hummer, and I can't honestly attest to his ability to do that." She smiled, but when Jordan didn't share in her joke she stared back at the fire. "So, anyway, I inherited the business. My father knew I was the only one with the balls to handle it. He'd been training me for years."

"He must have loved you very much to leave it to you."

"I don't know if I can live up to his expectations."

"I'm sure you're doing a great job." Support etched every syllable.

The fire licked at the air inside the fireplace. Kelsey watched the dancing flames. "I've done what was expected. It's hard to explain...complicated."

"Kelsey, I'm tired of playing games here. I know we started off as fuck partners, and God knows I never expected..."

Kelsey turned slowly, her heart hammering against her chest. *You never expected what?* She thought about her irrational attraction to Jordan and the feelings she'd tried to disown ever since they met. There was more than a sexual connection between them. She had stopped denying that. But she didn't know where Jordan stood.

"What didn't you expect?" she whispered hopefully.

Jordan grunted. "I never expected things to get so crazy. People busting up your house, death threats, that crazy woman in the club, police scrambling to protect you. Get to the point, Kelsey. I'm running out of patience."

Kelsey gasped. All the words she longed to say flew from her mind. She wanted to find out if Jordan had feelings for her, and she wanted to talk about the past two years. She wanted Jordan to know how sad she was that her father had died alone in his office and that she never got to say good-bye. How lost without her mother she was. How alone she'd felt as she stood over her father's grave, and how miserable her life had been. Until they met.

Kelsey held her breath, thinking about that incredible fact. Everything suddenly mattered more. The thought of losing Jordan was unbearable. She laced her fingers together nervously. How could she explain the craziness in her life without risking what meant more than anything? Until this moment she hadn't realized how desperately she needed Jordan to understand and accept her. She hadn't seen her own feelings for what they were.

Kelsey felt color surging into her cheeks. The breath she'd been holding rushed from her chest, making a sound like a whimper. She turned sharply to face Jordan, the truth trembling on her lips. She was in love.

"What kind of business do you fucking own?" Jordan's harsh words slapped reality in her face.

Shocked, she met Jordan's fiery glare and fought the urge to crawl into her lap and cry at the injustice that she would probably lose what she hadn't even known she wanted. "It's a corporation," she stammered, delaying what was to come.

"Well, that narrows it down."

Jordan's cynical expression rubbed her raw in places that were suddenly sensitive. Kelsey cursed inwardly. If only she'd put her plan into effect a long time ago. If only she'd been strong enough to face the greedy old men who wanted more money, as if their wallets weren't fat enough. Jordan would never hear her out. She'd never get the chance to explain what a decent, good-hearted person she really was.

What Jordan was about to hear would turn her stomach inside out, and Kelsey wouldn't have a chance to defend herself. How could she explain her decision to continue shredding companies and tossing out employees? How could she expect Jordan to forgive her for not changing course as soon as her father died? She could hardly forgive herself.

Kelsey lifted her chin. Her father had never let her down, and she'd be damned if she'd let him down now. She wasn't going to apologize for him. He'd built a successful business and lived the American Dream. People like Jordan came and went, but her father's memory and the life they'd shared would always be with her.

"I buy companies that aren't doing well," she said.

"Like that Riching woman's?"

"Yes, we buy weak companies, tear them apart, kick out the employees, and sell off the assets for more profit than you could ever fucking dream of."

"Now, *that* doesn't sound so nice."

Kelsey waited for what she knew would be coming. Jordan was just like the rest of the world. Her hardened face proved that. She watched the truth dawn.

"You've got to be fucking kidding me." Jordan slapped her palm against her forehead. "You're Billings Industries?" She rose, shaking her head.

Kelsey's heart jammed in her throat. She stared at Jordan's face, unable to think of anything that would make her look any less of the monster she was. Her protective mode was in full swing. To say yes was a trap, but to say no would put her right back in the path of lies she was desperately trying to avoid. Denial was pointless. Jordan would only have to Google the company's name and she would see Kelsey listed as the president. With all that had happened to Mrs. Porter, it surprised Kelsey that she hadn't done so already and joined the dots.

With every ounce of willpower she could muster, she said, "Yes. My father built Billings Industries and I took over from him as president."

"Oh, fuck." Jordan threw her hands in the air. "The person who owns the company that ruined my mother's life—the person who sent her to live in that garbage-reeking, drug-infested housing project is sitting in my damn living room."

Hatred beamed from the depths of her eyes. Kelsey knew that look. She'd seen it on hundreds of faces as she addressed groups of employees about to be laid off. She opened her mouth to defend herself then clamped it shut. If there was one thing she had left, it was pride. There wasn't a single thing she could say. Tears welled in her eyes. She desperately wanted to go to

Jordan, to hug her and tell her how sorry she was, but she stilled the impulse. She was used to this. The condemnation, the hatred. Once Jordan was done, she'd walk away numb.

She stood her ground. "Everyone we lay off receives a fair severance package."

"Is that what you call it?" Jordan folded her arms as though she needed to stop herself from throwing a punch. "You make me sick."

She stalked out of the room and a door slammed somewhere in the house.

Kelsey didn't move. Terrified and confused over what to do next, she tried to slow her shallow breathing and think about her options. She could go after Jordan and try to explain that everything was about to change at Billings, but what was the use? Jordan was just like everyone else, judging her before she knew the whole truth. How could she think Jordan would trust her enough to set aside her anger and listen to her plans.

She located her cell phone and scrolled to Artie's number. Before she could make the call, the door flew open and Jordan stormed in her direction. The fighter in Kelsey wouldn't allow her to flinch. She lifted her chin and faced Jordan's hard glare.

"I want you out of here first thing in the morning." Jordan's gaze raked over her face. Her lips curled into a snarl. She dropped a blanket and pillow at Kelsey's feet, then turned and left.

Kelsey flinched with the banging of the door. All she had to do was chase her, tell her the truth about her changes to the company, and the whole mess would be over. Shouldn't it be that simple? She took a few hesitant steps, then stopped.

Jordan was furious, and her rage was understandable. This was the wrong time to try to reason with her. Kelsey wasn't ready to hear Jordan say that John Billings was a cruel and heartless man. And if she talked about her reasons for changing the company's objectives, she would be admitting that she despised what he'd done, too. She'd be damned if anyone would force her to say that. He'd worked his ass off to create his dreams, after having that ass beat daily by a brutal father when he was a child. She couldn't dishonor him, no matter what.

Tears slipped from her eyes.

Jordan would never know the truth.

Jordan paced around her bedroom, fists clenched at her side. She'd never wanted to punch someone so badly. Dear God, how could she not have put two and two together? Kelsey Billings, owner of Billings Industries, was in her house. She'd slept with her, for Pete's sake.

She slumped on the edge of the bed and rested her head in her hands. An image of Kelsey, naked in her arms, slithered through her mind. Jordan could feel that beautiful body quivering while she drove her fingers deep inside. Her shoulders still bore the sense memory of those delicate arms wrapped around her neck, holding on to her like they'd never get another chance at such joy.

She pushed off the bed, stomped into the bathroom, and stared at her reflection. "Can you fucking believe your luck?"

She turned away from the mirror, doused the light, and went back in the bedroom. After tugging her shirt over her head and yanking off her jeans, she donned a pair of boxers and slid into bed. A pang gripped her heart when she heard the faint sound of Kelsey crying. Had she been too mean to her?

Hell no. This woman had ruined her mother's life and sent her into depression. She didn't owe Kelsey an ounce of an apology. If anything, she should offer to meet her on the mat.

"Cry all night long. I don't give a fuck," Jordan said.

She flicked off the lamp and darkness surrounded her, bringing vivid images crashing through her brain. She tossed and turned, trying to push the explicit memories aside, finding no end to the torture. Knowing Kelsey was in the room along the hall, possibly naked under the blanket, tortured her further.

Perhaps she had been too harsh. Kelsey was obviously very close to her father, and Jordan admired her fierce loyalty. But that was no excuse. She could have sold the business if she objected to its activities, if she had a fucking heart and thought people deserved better than to be treated as trash.

Jordan tried to imagine herself in the same position, inheriting a monster from a father she loved. Maybe she wouldn't have been able to let go, either. Was it fair of her to judge Kelsey when she hadn't faced a decision like that herself? Jordan rolled her eyes that she was trying to make excuses for a woman who knowingly destroyed lives.

Kelsey was a witch. A witch in the most scrumptious body she'd ever seen.

Jordan growled and sat up in the bed as a horrible reality dawned on her. "Oh, shit. I'm in love with a witch."

Before she could change her mind, she eased out of bed and crept along the hallway to the great room, expecting to find Kelsey sniffling and shaking.

But the couch was empty. Kelsey was gone.

Chapter Eleven

Jordan oozed like melted chocolate through Kelsey's thoughts. If she gave this up, she might never be able to have someone to love and cherish for the rest of her life. Tears streamed down her face and sobs shook her body. Could she have Jordan? Was there a chance that Jordan would cool off and be willing to look at both sides of the story?

She stared out at the blur of lights beyond the car window. Did she really want someone who would always disapprove of her life, even if she made changes? Could she trust someone who saw her as a monster? It wasn't her fault companies couldn't stay afloat. If Billings didn't take them over, some other large corporation would. Most of the owners of the companies they bought were thankful to be saved from bankruptcy hell.

She glanced sideways at Artie, drawing comfort from his strong profile. "Thank you for picking me up." She wiped her face, but fresh tears flowed fast and furious.

"Honey, when you stepped into your daddy's shoes, you knew it would be tough letting people into your life. Your own mother was living proof. She thought your daddy was a monster, but she was in love with him. She would have done anything just to be near him."

"At least he had someone. As long as I own this business I'm never going to find anyone."

"Oh, honey. You're going to find love one day. You just have to choose someone who can handle what you do for a living."

"They won't have to. I'm selling Billings Industries."

Artie eased off the accelerator. "You're what? When did you decide this?"

"I've been thinking about it for a while. I'm going to walk away and never look back. I have to."

He drove in silence for a short time, then said, "I think it's the best decision you've ever made in your life."

"Daddy's probably rolling over in his grave this very second. I hate to think I'm letting him down."

Artie gave a soft chuckle. "I doubt that. He'd be proud that you're going after what you really want instead of burying yourself in his dreams."

Kelsey shook her head uncertainly. "I don't know about that. He always wanted me to run the business."

"Because he knew you could. He wanted you to be strong and independent. But miserable? Nope, not John. He loved you."

"I know." Kelsey smiled sadly.

Artie gave her hand a pat. "He once told me something I think you need to hear. He said he'd give up every dime he'd ever earned to have your mother look at him the way she did when they were newlyweds. He said her fire was gone, but her passion kept her there watching over him. He was devastated when she left."

Kelsey stared at him. His words were foreign. Her father had never spoken kindly about her mother. But still, she knew they'd loved each other. Even though they no longer kissed or hugged by the time she was a teen, the love still floated around them. Kelsey had always felt it when they were near each other.

And now, to sit here with Artie telling her exactly how much they had meant to each other, she felt dazed. To think that her father would've been willing to toss everything to the wind for that love was more breathtaking than she could have imagined.

"Why didn't he give up the business for her?" The question was out of her mouth before she could stop it. "If he would have been happier."

"He was a fool, and I never missed a chance to tell him," Artie replied flatly. "He was never sure if giving up the money and the power would win back her heart."

"He believed in taking care of his family," Kelsey said in his defense.

"But he destroyed it instead." Artie slowed down and steered into the line of traffic taking the next exit. "He could have given up the business and lived off his bank account for the rest of his life. He could have given your mother what she wanted and still achieved what he'd set out to do."

Kelsey sighed. She had heard her parents arguing about that, her mother asking how many millions it would take to bury the past. Her father had grown up in poverty with a brutal father and always swore he would never let his family suffer as he had. Kelsey respected him for that, and she knew she'd inherited his deep sense of responsibility. No matter what Kevin did, she was always there for him. If she could find her mother, she would be there for her, too.

"Billings Industries became his first love when he realized he'd lost your mother," Artie said. "He thought it was too late to get her back."

"What do you think?"

They turned into the Whitakers' neighborhood, a sea of family homes with tidy gardens and swimming pools in their backyards.

"I think he made the worst mistake of his life not going after her."

Kelsey stared at him, lights flashing in her head as her plans for the company rolled through her mind. She was more determined than ever to see this through to the end, to set Billings Industries on a new course of action, to never hurt another living soul to feed corporate greed. Maybe once she was done, she would go find Jordan and they could start all over.

She gave Artie her best smile. "Thank you for sharing my father's fears with me. I don't want to live my life loving my second love. This company wasn't my dream. I want my own."

"That's my girl. I'm proud of you."

She plucked a tissue from the box on the seat and patted her wet face. "Don't be proud yet. It's going to be hell to make sure this company gets into the right hands."

Douglas slipped into her mind. Of course. How could she have been so stupid? All those grueling hours he'd spent with her going over figures, sleepless nights trying to figure out how the company could help struggling companies survive and keep their employees out of the unemployment line. Douglas knew what she wanted to do. He knew every corner of the business. There were no other hands she would ever trust more with her father's dreams.

"Douglas!" she yelled in excitement. "Douglas can take over."

"Now I know you've lost your mind," Artie said. "My son might be good at his job, but running a company as big as Billings Industries is another story."

"Are you crazy? He helped me come up with the plan to turn it all around. I know he can do this."

"Can I ask you something?"

Kelsey froze. That fatherly tone that always made her stand at attention. "Sure."

"If you knew you wanted to turn things around, and if you spent so much time figuring out how to do just that, why didn't you do it yourself?"

Kelsey's chin fell to her chest. "I was afraid I'd screw things up and make the company fold. I couldn't bear it if I destroyed his dreams."

"So you're both fools?"

She smiled uncertainly and shrugged. "In a way, I guess so. Lucky for me, I'm young enough to get out and find a life."

They stopped in the Whitakers' driveway. Their house had been her second home ever since her mother left. Ellie, Artie's perfect wife, had helped her go through her mom's belongings when it became clear that she was never coming back. She'd done the same when her dad died.

It was almost like she'd lost both parents, Kelsey thought. She'd buried one and couldn't find the other. She didn't know which was worse. At least she could visit her father's grave. She'd saved a few select things that reminded her of her mother, but they could never take the place of the real thing.

Ellie met her at the front door and gave Artie a wave as he pulled out of the driveway, returning to duty. Even at this late hour, she wore her apron. Laugh lines crinkled around her deep blue eyes and her gray hair was twisted into curlers. Her pudgy face broke into a grin the closer Kelsey got to her. Those welcoming arms spread open for a hug and Kelsey slid into them, feeling her heartache and troubles drain. No matter what her problems were, Ellie always helped her get a new perspective. She'd hug her, then bring her cookies and milk, as if that was the cure for every real or perceived ailment. Usually, it was.

Giving Kelsey's hand a gentle squeeze, she said, "I have cookies."

"That's just what I need. More weight."

"Oh, girl. Give me a break. What I wouldn't give to have a figure like yours." Ellie bundled her into the kitchen. They sat on padded chairs at the glass dining table. "Do you think they would let some old fart with cauliflower thighs do a sexy dance at your club?"

Kelsey choked on the cookie.

"What?" Ellie glanced down at her handlebar hips. "Think I'd be too heavenly for them?"

"I don't think we have enough bouncers to hold the audience off you." Kelsey gave her a wink.

It was the best feeling in the world to have someone on her side, loving her no matter what. She recalled the time she'd admitted to Ellie that she was a lesbian. Ellie's eyebrows had arched with the confession. "You say this like you have a disease or something. Don't say it like you're ashamed. If you think a little word like 'lesbian' is going to make me love you any less, you've got another thought coming."

Kelsey's heart ached with the memory. She couldn't love Ellie an ounce more for all the support she'd given through Kelsey's heartaches.

"It's good to be here," she sighed. "You've no idea what a lousy month I've had."

"I'm sorry, sweetie. What's happening?"

"Oh, just the usual. Work. More work." Kelsey felt pretty sure Artie wouldn't have mentioned the vandalism at her house. He didn't like to worry his wife.

Ellie studied her face intently. "You lie so sweet."

Kelsey glared at her. "I hate how you can read my mind."

"I know," Ellie said with satisfaction. "Tell me about this new love of yours."

Kelsey froze. Was it written on her face or something? She'd only just figured it out for herself, and maybe she was wrong about the feelings that kept her stomach in knots. She'd programmed herself not to feel love, not to need it, not to want it. Fuck. Was it love that kept Jordan playing through her mind like a virtual reality?

"There's not much to tell," she said weakly.

"Oh, bull. Artie said sparks were shooting off the two of you."

So he *had* told Ellie a few details. Kelsey didn't feel like admitting that she'd probably ruined her chances of a real relationship, so she gave a shrug. "I just met her recently. It's no big deal."

"Child, who do you think you're talking to? You haven't dated a soul since your father died. If you're seeing this woman, then you've flopped in the love barrel."

"It's not like that. We were just…casual."

"Uh-huh. So, when exactly did you know you were in love with her?"

Jordan flashed through her mind. She balled her hands so hard around the cookie she'd taken, it crumbled.

"I don't know what I feel," she admitted. "But it doesn't matter. I blew it."

"Then you better fix it." Ellie looked up at the wall clock. She always cooked a meal when Artie worked a late shift so he'd have hot food waiting for him at home.

Automatically, Kelsey went to the fridge and found bacon and eggs. They started preparing food together like there was nothing strange about cooking breakfast in the middle of the night.

"I don't think it's fixable," she said, slicing bread for thick French toast. "Turns out her mother fell victim to one of my company's shutdowns."

Ellie shook her head. "Doesn't matter. Fix it."

"Why would I want a woman who hates me?"

"She won't after you fix it." Ellie cracked eggs into a bowl.

"And how am I supposed to fix it?"

Ellie found the whisk. "You're one of the smartest people I know. You run that big company all by yourself. You'll think of something."

No way. She didn't need love. Nor was this ache in the pit of her stomach an indication she'd truly found it, or that she'd let it slip through her fingers.

"Ellie, she hates me, and I can't blame her. Besides, as I said before, I'm not in love with her."

"Don't make me cuss this early in the morning." Ellie thrashed the hell out of the eggs. "If you don't find a way to patch this up, I might have to cut off your cookies and milk."

Kelsey didn't answer. Ellie didn't know her as well as she thought she did. *I don't beg, and I sure as hell don't plead.* She heated the iron skillet and placed a couple of pieces of toast on to cook.

"I want to meet her," Ellie said.

"That probably won't happen."

She should have known better than to argue. Ellie slapped some bacon on the grilling tray and asked, "What's her name?"

"Jordan Porter." Snippily, Kelsey added, "And she's in the phone book. Call her and ask her what she thinks of me. Then you'll understand why this can't be fixed."

"We'll see," Ellie replied.

"Be my guest." Kelsey flipped the toast. She liked having the last word with Ellie. It was a rare event.

CHAPTER TWELVE

Jordan slipped into the shower to remove the sweat from her exhausted body. She ached in places that hadn't felt pain in years. She was behind in her training and paying for it now as the hot water attempted to ease her screaming muscles. And now that she was thinking about sweat, aching muscles, and training, she realized her fire for the sport was almost gone.

There'd been no life in her this morning as she attempted to punch and kick Kelsey from her mind. Her mornings alone in the empty studio used to make her feel alive and ready for any opponent, but she couldn't care less now. Was it time to hang up her belt and give this game a rest? She seriously needed to figure out what she wanted to do with the rest of her life. She had enough money to live comfortably for a while if the karate shop remained open and doing as well as it was.

A guy she'd met had offered to franchise the business and team with her to establish a brand of clothing and equipment. She wouldn't have to work another day for the rest of her life if she took a deal like that one. But sitting around doing nothing wasn't what she wanted, either.

She shoved her face under the pounding stream. There were too many other things to think about right now. She needed to get Kelsey Billings out of her mind, for good. The three-dimensional images were winning by a landslide, preventing her from focusing on the decisions she needed to make. About her mother. Work. Everything.

And to think she'd been planning to tell Kelsey she loved her.

Had she been too cruel? Could she have handled things differently? No. She hadn't been too cruel. Kelsey was a monster in a gorgeous body. She didn't owe her any apologies. She was better off to have said her piece now, when she could walk away without having her heart torn out. Jordan was thankful she hadn't been any deeper into the relationship.

She let the thoughts stew in her brain while she locked the karate shop door. She'd left a message for the staff, telling them she wouldn't be in for a few days. Lord knew what she was going to do with the time. Maybe a road trip was in order, anything to vacate her mind and mend her soul. She dropped down into the Viper and cranked the radio to avoid thinking. A slow, grinding song poured out, and a tantalizing image of Kelsey filled her mind. The streets were deserted at this early morning hour, giving her nothing to concentrate on but that stunning body and those gorgeous eyes filling with tears while Jordan screamed at her.

She reminded herself that it was Kelsey's fault she was losing sleep and would probably lose the match that was supposed to be the final seal on her reputation before she officially retired. It was Kelsey's fault her mother was in dire straits. Even the fire burning between her thighs was Kelsey's fault.

Jordan wished she'd never walked into The Pink Lady that night. She wished she had asked some obvious questions sooner. But maybe she didn't want to know the truth. Maybe she had ignored her uneasy suspicions because she wanted Kelsey so badly.

She swore out loud and forced herself to pay attention to the traffic around her. If she wanted any peace of mind, she couldn't think about that pretty demon for another second.

❖

Kelsey stood outside the white brick building that had stolen her father away from her mother, and said, "Today I hand you over to someone who will take very good care of you. I promise."

A thought occurred to her as she passed through security, her heels clicking against the marble floor. How would it feel to stop hanging on to dreams that weren't hers to begin with? Even the air around her had changed. The smell of the building didn't seem as potent. The echo of her heels on the marble didn't sound evil. She felt free.

She quickened her steps. Today she would start putting things into motion formally. Soon she would hand over her father's baby and walk away. A smile stole across her face as she pushed open the heavy doors to the conference room. The men turned to stare at her. One looked at his watch and arched an eyebrow in silent disapproval. She was late. Again.

Kelsey had always dreaded coming here to tear down another company, another life, another happy home. Glancing around the room, she wondered what would happen when she laid out the proposal. Some of the associates would probably refuse to have any part of the changes, but she hoped she could persuade a majority to lend their support.

"Good morning, gentlemen." She shrugged out of her jacket. Lifting the key documents from her briefcase, she said, "I've called this meeting to discuss the future of Billings Industries."

"Kelsey?" Douglas started.

She held up her hand to quiet him. "I know what I'm doing." She turned to the other men. "Gentlemen. Before I get started, I want to thank each and every one of you for the time you've put into this company. Some of your faces I've seen since I was a little girl, and I've looked up to you as people my father depended on. Today I come to you to ask that you support me in a very hard decision. A few days ago I decided to sell Billings Industries."

Gasps echoed around the room while hard gazes locked on her. Kelsey let the shock of her words sink in, and then continued.

"However, selling this company my father worked his ass off to build isn't what I want. It would only wind up in hands that could do damage."

She let their mutters calm, then moved to the window overlooking the beautiful city. The bright sun cast a yellow haze over the high-rise buildings. "Instead I've decided to place the company into hands I can trust. Douglas Whitaker will be taking control, starting Monday."

Douglas gasped. "What? Have you lost your mind?"

"No. You know exactly what I want to do. You know the game plan from A to Z. Douglas, I trust you, and I trust these men. If you won't do it then I'll have to sell, and I swear I'll never look back."

One of the men cleared his throat. "Kelsey, please reconsider this. Your father wanted this business to always stay the same."

"No, he didn't. My father was a fool for many years over things you wouldn't understand. But I'm going to change the things he didn't have the guts to."

The man's mouth dropped open. "You can't possibly mean that. Your father was a tiger in that chair."

"I am as well," she said with more confidence than she knew she possessed. "My father made mistakes and I don't intend to repeat them. So we're moving in a new direction."

Douglas rose from his chair and wrapped his arms around her. His dark hair rested against her cheek. "I'm proud of you."

She gave him a smile. "I knew you would be. If there is anyone here that would rather quit instead of seeing this company take a different approach, please feel free to turn in your resignation by the end of the day."

She glanced around, waiting for the men to jump to their feet and race from the room.

One of the senior associates asked, "What kind of new direction are you talking about?"

"I don't want this company to hurt another living soul." Kelsey slammed her fist down on the table. "I want it helping companies get back on their feet. I want us to walk hand in hand with them if we have to. Finance new projects. Invest in good ideas."

"You want Billings to become a venture capitalist?" A dignified old man looked appalled.

"Why not? We have some of the smartest men in the world right here in this room. We can do this."

Douglas smoothed down his tie. "I think we all know there are many different ways to approach this idea, and not all of them involve throwing money at computer nerds who want to try out gimmicks on the Internet."

This raised a ripple of laughter. Douglas knew how to bring their colleagues on board. She was counting on that.

"You've all worked hard to make this company what it is," she said. "Your ideas are going to be invaluable as we move forward."

"Kelsey and I have been working on a proposal," Douglas said. "That's probably a good starting point for our discussions today."

He handed a document to his assistant and asked for copies.

"If you don't need me here," Kelsey murmured in his ear, "I have something important to take care of."

"What about the legal stuff?"

"You're the boss now," she teased. "Get everything drawn up and I'll sign."

"I'll make sure you come out of this looking good," he promised.

"That'll be a change for me." Planting a quick kiss on his cheek, she said, "Thank you. I know you'll do a great job."

She left the room a brand-new person, floating higher than any cloud ever could. Billings Industries was moving toward new goals. She only wished she'd made this decision a long time ago instead of fearing her father's contemporaries would look down on her and walk away. There was only one thing more she needed to do before she left for the day. She found Sarah, the personnel manager, and handed her a set of instructions. They had a brief discussion, Kelsey made a few phone calls, then she locked the door to her office.

She smiled to herself as she stepped out into the afternoon sunlight. *I think Daddy would be proud of me. I'm doing what he couldn't.*

❖

Jordan flattened a stack of T-shirts in the bag she was packing. Her cell phone vibrated against her hip. This time she checked the caller ID and resigned herself to another difficult conversation.

"Mom, you have to stop calling me every five minutes. I'm busy."

Deafening screams erupted from her mother. Not one word was audible.

Jordan's heart leapt to her throat. She knew she should have listened to her voice mail. "Mom, I can't understand you. Calm down. What's wrong?"

Silence replaced the screams.

Panicking, Jordan asked, "Are you okay, Mom? Do I need to call 911?"

"Yes, I'm having a heart attack." He mother instantly hooted and said, "I'm kidding. I got a job. Oh, my God. I got a job." She squealed with happiness.

"Jeez, Mom. You scared the shit out of me."

"Poop."

"What?"

"Don't say 'shit' to your mother. Say 'poop.'"

"Okay, Mom. So tell me about this job."

"I don't really know a lot yet. The kind lady said she read my work history with McGregor and I'm exactly what she's looking for. She wanted to hire me on the spot. I have a really good feeling about this, baby."

"Don't you even get an interview?" Though Jordan was thrilled, she was also skeptical.

"Nope. And you're going to shit when you hear how much I'm going to be making. But I'm not going to jinx myself, so I'll tell you later. But I will give you a hint. I can move out of this dump with my first paycheck." She gave another squeal of delight.

"Poop." Jordan couldn't resist the urge to play tit for tat.

"What, honey?"

"Don't say 'shit' to your daughter. Say 'poop.'"

Her mother chuckled. "I love you, baby. I gotta go. Wish me luck."

"Wait, Mom. What's the name of the company?"

The phone was already dead. Jordan flipped it shut and tossed it on the bed beside her bag. Frowning, she folded a pair of jeans. She'd left her mother's name with several employment agencies after striking out with all the companies she'd called. But she hadn't, in all honesty, been optimistic. Today she'd even made the decision that she was going to move her mother out of the projects, whether she liked it or not. First she would take a few days to herself, then she would come back and arrange a moving company.

Kelsey ripped through her mind. If only she'd handled things differently with her. If only she'd let Kelsey explain herself instead of slapping her with all the blame, she might be lucky in love right now instead of feeling miserable and guilty.

Jordan punched the edge of the bed.

CHAPTER THIRTEEN

Kelsey stared at the vacant house across the street for a few seconds, then let herself in her front door.

What kind of game was Paula playing with her? After Artie had the breakfast she and Ellie cooked, he'd told her the rest of the bad news. Not only was Paula her new neighbor, but her construction company had been working on the Whitakers' house. They'd just finished building a large den where Artie could entertain his buddies around a pool table. Paula had been present throughout the job. While she was building the new addition, she'd heard all about Kelsey over dinners and drinks with Ellie.

Artie was not only shocked, he was scared. His eyes had glazed over in dismay. Kelsey wasn't sure who she hated more for his self-blame, herself or Paula. As much as she would like to be scared out of her mind, somehow she wasn't. Somehow, she just knew Paula wasn't behind the death threats, despite her behavior at the club. She visualized Paula's seductive smile. She'd left no doubt as to what she'd wanted from Kelsey. Had Jordan not been there, Kelsey might have been obliged to ease some of Paula's tension by quenching her own sexual thirst. But her mind had been on Jordan and Jordan alone. Paula's fingers were not the ones she wanted inside her thong, ready to rip a scream of pleasure from her.

Kelsey leaned forward on the couch, pushing the arousing thoughts from her mind. That relationship was over now. Why in the hell did she let herself continue to dwell on it? Plucking the phone from the cradle on the end table, she studied the number Artie had scribbled down for her, along with the new security codes. She set her phone to record the call as he'd instructed, and dialed Paula's number. She was suddenly unsure of what to say when Paula picked up.

"Is this Paula Riching?"

"Yes. What can I do for you?"

Artie wanted her to get an admission, if possible. "You can start by telling me why you trashed my house."

"I'm sorry? Who is this?"

"Kelsey. Kelsey Billings."

A soft chuckle oozed over the line. "Well, well. And to what do I owe this pleasure? I've heard such great things about the real Kelsey. Sugar sweet, with a heart of gold. Ellie thinks you walk on water."

"Did you trash my house, you fucking freak?"

"If I say yes, will you let me come over and help you clean it up?" Her voice was calm and crystal clear with want. "I *do* know where you live."

Kelsey felt immediate confusion. If Paula did the damage and wrote the message on her porch, she was the crazy stalker behind the death threats. But she sure sounded sane, and terribly horny, exactly like she'd sounded at the bar.

"Screw you," Kelsey said coldly.

"I was trying to, but you almost broke my fingers."

"Yes, I remember." Kelsey smiled, recalling the pain that replaced Paula's lusty look as her fingers were bent backward. If looks could really kill, she would've been dead on contact when she pushed Paula away that night.

Cupping the cordless phone against her ear, she walked to the window to look out over the lawn, admiring the large three-story house that had sat vacant for the past two years across the street. Someone had been working on the yard, getting it ready to be occupied. Paula would be moving in soon, from the looks of it.

"Invite me over," Paula said

"Yeah, right. Do you think I'm stupid?"

"Pretend you are and invite me over."

"I don't think so."

"Your loss, sweet stuff. I could have made it very enjoyable."

Kelsey had no doubt she could deliver on that promise. She'd seen the desire striving in those deep blue eyes. "You can meet me for coffee. Public place, crowded surroundings."

"If that'll make you feel better." Paula laughed.

Kelsey wasn't sure anything would make her feel safe, but for some reason, she had to see Paula's eyes when she denied the notes and the vandalism. She'd been trained to keep her enemies close and deal with threats directly. Being face-to-face with a woman who could easily cause her harm might boost her confidence. And if she could rule Paula out as a likely suspect, Artie and Ellie wouldn't have to feel bad about being open with her.

"Thirty minutes at Los Santos," Kelsey said.

Artie would kill her if he knew what she was doing. He had only asked her to have a phone conversation with Paula to see if she could be trapped into an admission. However, he didn't seem convinced Paula was behind the threats, and Kelsey trusted his instincts.

She picked up her car keys and strode out of her house. Nothing could lower her spirits after her triumphant departure from Billing Industries, not even the freshly scrubbed threat that still left a faint imprint on her porch.

❖

Paula was leaning against a huge white Chevy Silverado when Kelsey pulled into the parking lot. She looked even sexier than she had at the bar. Her tanned arms extended from under a white T-shirt, reminding Kelsey of how strong they felt grabbing her that night. Air hoses, a set of sawhorses, and other construction equipment took up space in the bed of her truck. A large magnet bearing the Riching Construction logo was affixed to a side panel.

Kelsey looked out over the crowded city streets at the cars lining up behind the red lights and the pedestrians awaiting the flashing hand to signal them across the street. She forced herself to match Paula's smile.

"Give me one good reason why I shouldn't call the cops about you."

Paula's bright white teeth appeared between her lips. "Because you're curious. You wouldn't be here for any other reason."

Kelsey shifted to her other foot, glaring at her, feeling stupid. She felt like her life had been opened like a book and pored over by this woman. There was no telling what Ellie had shared while she served her famous lasagna.

"Are you stalking me?" she asked.

"Could you blame me if I was? That sexy body. Who could resist?" Paula wiggled her eyebrows.

Kelsey folded her arms over her chest. Though all fear had vanished, something else remained, leaving her cautious and wary. Paula was unreadable.

"So," she asked cautiously. "Did you want to chat about something or stand in the parking lot all day?"

"Depends." Paula's eyes traveled slowly up and down Kelsey's prickling body. "Will I get to stare at you while the hot sun blazes down on us?"

Kelsey took in her loose jeans and the smudges of sawdust stuck to her T-shirt. What if she was dead wrong and Paula was good at hiding her true intentions? Or what if she'd just been having a bad day at The Pink Lady and was completely innocent?

"Come on, fraidy-cat. Let's go have lunch, get to know each other a little better. Seems we have a lot in common." Paula gestured toward the front door.

Keeping her guard up, Kelsey strolled into the restaurant with her. They found an empty booth and sat across from each other.

After the waitress took their drink orders, Paula said, "So you think I trashed your place?" She arched her eyebrows. "You have a beautiful house, by the way."

Kelsey tensed. "Thank you. In case you've forgotten, you *did* threaten me."

Paula leaned toward her, sliding her hand across to Kelsey's. The impulse to jerk back was immediate. Kelsey stilled the urge and forced herself to meet Paula's gaze. The last thing she wanted was for Paula to realize she wasn't as confident as she appeared. As a matter of fact, she was pretty well scared shitless.

"My behavior was uncalled for." Paula's face was serious. "Embarrassed women do tend to fly off the handle. I apologize for calling you a bitch."

Kelsey shook her head. "I *am* a bitch. That part didn't bother me." She smiled grimly when Paula laughed. "Your threat did."

"Oh, I meant that part about remembering my face. I figured if I came back and behaved myself, you might give me another lap dance. Not that my heart could stand another one." She released Kelsey's hand. "I'm sorry if I scared you, and I'm also sorry I wasn't able to chase away your nuisance of a fan."

Kelsey eyed her. "What are you talking about? What fan?"

"The one I was paid to make jealous."

"Excuse me? Someone paid you to scare away a customer?" Every fine strand of hair on the back of her neck stood on edge.

"The bartender said you were trying to get rid of that tall, dark-haired woman who came to sit with you. She paid me a hundred bucks to get a lap dance from you. Said if I played my cards right, I might stand a chance for a date as well as chasing away your admirer. Instead, I let my hands overpower my common sense and got my ass kicked out."

Kelsey's mind automatically snapped back to that night. Phyllis, the regular bartender, was behind the bar. Sharon was helping out, too. Anger sliced through her gut. That bitch! Would Sharon stoop to such a level to get back at her? Kelsey remembered the way she'd slammed her hand down, scaring the shit out of her and telling her it was time to dance.

"Uh-oh. I take it you had no idea."

Kelsey shook her head. Sharon would get a piece of her mind as soon as she got back to The Pink Lady. And, if she was willing to stoop so low, would she stoop even lower and make up the phone calls and death threats? Her fear eased with the knowledge. She could handle the known, it was the unknown that worried her.

"By the way," Paula drawled. "I wanted to thank you for ripping my dad's business apart." Her smile slid from her face.

Kelsey's heart leapt to her throat.

Chapter Fourteen

What were the odds that a Billings takeover had actually made someone happy? It gave her a thrill to hear that Paula's father had been relieved to walk away and retire with his head held high. No wonder he'd signed those papers so quickly. He'd been ready for the end.

Kelsey punched in the new code for the gate and drove through the grounds, wearing a huge smile. Paula said she'd been ecstatic when the offer came in. It had been a dream come true for her family, since her father was on the verge of a nervous breakdown. The sale gave him the freedom to retire and Paula the courage and cash to buy out the Riching Construction subsidiary. How sad that her father hadn't lived to see her make such a big success of the business, or to enjoy the freedom of a comfortable retirement.

Paula had explained how he'd mourned the death of her mother and never gotten over her long battle with cancer. He'd pounced on their offer just to grasp a fresh start. As soon as she heard the story, Kelsey knew she'd made the right decision about Billings Industries. If she'd taken the easy way out and sold the company, she would have regretted it. Instead she would have the power to make a difference in people's lives.

She parked in front of the house and looked around before she got out of the Explorer. For safety, Artie wanted her to park in the garage and use the internal door, but she refused to change her habits because some jerk wanted to scare her.

She walked inside and checked messages on the answering machine, drooping when the voice she longed to hear was missing. She wondered what Jordan was doing. Was she thinking about her? Did she hate her as much as Kelsey thought? *Of course she does. You ruined her mother's life. Stop thinking about her, you dork.* Jordan was gone. The sooner she adjusted to that fact, the better. She didn't share Ellie's confidence that the relationship could be "fixed." Even if Jordan was willing to talk, Kelsey wasn't prepared to grovel. If she couldn't be accepted for who she was, then they had nothing to discuss.

She slumped on the couch and returned a call from Darren. In his chatty message, he'd suggested a slumber party. Kelsey asked him to come over. While she waited for him to arrive at the gate, she fixed a plate of appetizers. She wasn't really in the mood to socialize, but she needed a distraction. Now that Paula Riching was out of contention, her mysterious stalker was still on the loose. She knew Sharon wouldn't hurt her. If she was the one making the threats, she was probably just trying to scare her into a live-in relationship. But until Artie arrested someone, Kelsey would be worried.

The buzzer sounded and Darren complained through the intercom, "Why'd you change the code? I feel like such an outsider."

"Until Artie catches this freak, I'm not giving it to anyone." Kelsey let him in and went out onto the porch as his Suzuki Samurai hurtled along the driveway. The tiny jeep fit his personality. Funny how cars fit the people who drove them.

He grabbed his bag from the passenger seat and skipped across the concrete. "Will you put cornrows in my hair?"

"Cornrows?"

"Don't give me that look." He slipped past her and into the house.

"But we have some scheming to do."

"First things first," Darren screamed from the living room. "Cornrows!"

Later, Kelsey twisted rows of hair over his head, creating a massive mess. "This looks like shit."

"That's because your hands are all shaky. What's gotten into you?" He turned in his chair to stare at her. "Is it that woman?"

"No, shithead. I'm not seeing her anymore." Kelsey flopped onto the couch. "Did you know Sharon paid the psycho from the bar to get a lap dance that night?"

"No way. The one you flattened behind the curtain? Sharon actually told you this?"

"Like she'd ever be brave enough." Kelsey rolled her eyes. "Paula told me."

"Who's Paula?" Darren unscrewed a bottle of nail polish and pulled her foot into his lap.

"The psycho. That was her name, remember? Paula Riching."

His gaze shot up to her. "You've seen her?"

"Turns out, Artie knows her. I had lunch with her today. And guess what? She's moving in across the street."

Darren's eyes narrowed. "She bought that house?" He looked around the room as if waiting for someone to jump out. "So, exactly why did you invite me over here? Did you just not want to die alone?"

She giggled. "She's cool. We had a great conversation." She stuffed cotton wool between her toes. "Do you think Sharon's behind the death threats?"

He didn't seem surprised by the question. "Wouldn't surprise me. She's obsessing over you." He dunked the brush a few times, then proceeded to polish her toenails a berry color. "I'm never around when she gets the calls. She's never around when I get them. And no one's ever seen anyone enter the bar to leave any notes. Furthermore, where was she while your house was being pillaged? Remember, she didn't come to the diner. She supposedly had other plans."

Kelsey focused on her toes. "But why? Why would she go to so much trouble to scare me?"

"To get you back."

"I was never hers."

"Not because she didn't want you to be, honey." He added another coat. "You haven't seen the way she watches you while you're up on that stage. She's crazy in love."

Kelsey stared at his slumped head, letting his statement roll around in her brain. Sharon was really freaked out over Jordan, but was she desperate enough to pull something like this? The thought of her tossing toilet paper around and breaking windows didn't fit right. Sharon wasn't a violent person.

"It can't be her. It just can't be." Kelsey let her head fall back on the cushions and stared at the ceiling. She couldn't completely discount the possibility. "How am I going to prove it?"

Darren never looked up from his creation. "Psychos always hang themselves. They're too stupid not to. Give her time."

Long after her toes and nails had been polished and Kelsey and Darren had watched several movies, Kelsey lay in bed and thought about Darren's comments.

Sharon always said she was a lover, not a fighter. And she'd proved her words true with skilled hands. Their sex had been sweaty and hot, lasting long into the wee hours of the mornings. So why didn't Kelsey love her? The question shot through her mind like a rocket. There was something lacking with Sharon. She could never put her finger on it.

While she struggled for the answer, Jordan stepped into her mind. Thick, dark hair. Washboard abs. Long, lean legs. Kelsey wanted to reach out and grab her and never let go. Her heart thudded into catapults. That's what was lacking with Sharon. And everyone else, for that matter. No sweaty palms, no fluttering heartbeats, and sure as hell no romantic thoughts.

Kelsey was in love, yet she'd allowed love to pass her by. Was she to blame? Did it matter now who was to blame? She'd stepped into her father's shoes and done a damn good job, even in her personal life. She snuggled her head into the pillow and willed her torturous thoughts to leave her alone. The images started, one flash at a time, continuing faster until a movie rolled behind her closed lids. Jordan closed the space between them, clamping her lips over Kelsey's. Heat spiraled between Kelsey's legs as the carousel rolled faster. Jordan's soft tongue melded with hers.

Kelsey slid a hand down and curled her finger over her clit. She ground her hips against her palm as she imagined Jordan's fingers inside her. She was soaked. Her nipples scraped against the soft sheet that clung to her. She forced her eyes open and threw her body to a sitting position. She focused on the dark ceiling and tried to talk sense into herself.

"Do *not* let her have this control. Get it together, Kelsey."

Yep, that would do it.

She threw a pillow across the room. No one had ever had so much power over her. She resented it, but she also felt awe. Love meant she couldn't shut down. Or distance herself. Or feel numb. How was she supposed to function?

The next morning, Kelsey was vigorously brushing her teeth when the phone rang.

"Get that," she mumbled as loud as she could to Darren. If it was Artie, she didn't want to miss the call.

When the phone continued to ring, she spit the foam in the sink and ran into her bedroom to grab the receiver from the nightstand. Her blood chilled at the sound of Jordan's sexy voice.

"Can we talk?"

Kelsey controlled her impulse to slam the phone down. The lump in her throat blocked all words.

"Are you there?" Jordan asked.

"Uh-huh."

"Kelsey, I'm going out of town and I wanted to say—"

"What?" Kelsey wasn't in the mood to listen to a lecture about her character flaws. "That I'm an ass for doing what I was trained to do, for making myself rich by putting someone else out of a job. I've heard it all, Jordan. Please, take your comments to hell and don't dial my number again." She slammed the phone down and threw the toothbrush against the wall. "Bitch."

"Whew, I guess you told someone." Darren jumped on the bed, making her body bounce on the mattress. "Was that Hunky Woman?"

"Yes. No. I mean, yes, it was her. But she's not hunky, she's a bitch."

"Well, pardon me." He pretended to be wounded. "You've got it bad, girl, I don't give a shit what you say."

Kelsey slid off the bed. "I do *not*."

"Okay." He seductively ran his fingers over the cotton comforter. "But I bet you thought of her last night while you were all alone in this bed, huh?" He shoved his lips against the pillow and made an awesome attempt at sounding like he was having sex with it.

Kelsey rolled her eyes and threw open the closet door.

"What exactly did she do to you? I forget."

"Blamed me for her family's misfortune." Kelsey held a tan blouse up to her chest and looked it over in the mirror against the back wall.

"Is there a possibility she was calling to say she's sorry?"

Kelsey stuck her head out of the closet to glare at him.

He held his hands up defensively. "I'm just saying—"

"I don't give a shit why she called." Kelsey flounced toward her dressing table. "And I don't want to talk about her anymore. I have a business to tend to and a future to get on with."

❖

Susan Porter was an older version of Jordan. Laugh lines etched the skin around her gorgeous green eyes. She had a radiant smile and a confident walk. The resemblance was uncanny.

Kelsey took a deep breath and tried to calm her pounding heart. Would Jordan be furious, or would she be grateful? It wasn't like Kelsey could compensate every person who'd fallen victim to her company, but this one meant the world to her. Even if she had no intention of seeing Jordan again, making amends to Mrs. Porter was a start in the right direction. She plastered a smile on her face and closed the distance between them.

"I'm so glad you decided to take our offer." She met the woman's firm grip and gave a gentle squeeze. "Please have a seat, Mrs. Porter."

"Call me Susan." She settled into the chair Kelsey indicated. "I was a little shocked, you understand. It was your company that put me out of a job."

Kelsey sat down. "Yes, ma'am, and I can't tell you how sorry I am about that situation. However, this company hasn't ever set out to hurt anyone. We buy sick and struggling businesses, ones that would flounder anyway. You would've been without a job either way. I do hope you understand."

Susan eyed her curiously. "I do. That's why I'm here."

Kelsey's heart lightened. "I'm so happy to hear that." She gave her a bright smile. "I have your papers ready. Since you've already spoken with Sarah about your pay and your new job title, do you have any other questions?"

"As a matter of fact, I do." Susan lifted the pitcher from the coffee table next to her and poured a glass of water. "Do you like children?"

Kelsey was taken aback. What in the hell did that have to do with anything? "Yes, I do."

"That's great. I want to be a grandmother one day."

"That's wonderful. I hope you have lots of them." Kelsey had a quick impulse to fire this woman before she ever hired her. Maybe Susan Porter was wacko. She should thank her lucky stars Jordan was out of her life in case she wound up just like her mother.

"I hope I do, too."

Kelsey slid the contract across the desk. "I'll need you to look this over and sign at the bottom of each page. If you have any questions, please feel free to ask."

"I do have another question, as a matter of fact."

Kelsey cringed. What in the world would this woman think to ask now?

"Why did you pick me? Out of all those fresh, new faces and brilliant minds, why me?" She held up her hand. "Never mind, don't answer that. I have a feeling you wouldn't tell me the truth."

This woman wasn't wacko at all. Kelsey's guard went up immediately. There was more to Susan than met the eye. She was a smart cookie, no doubt about it.

"Some things in life don't have an answer, Susan, no matter how hard we try to understand."

Jordan's mother seemed pleased with the reply. Her radiant smile lit up. She signed the contract and pushed it back across Kelsey's desk.

"You can start next Monday," Kelsey said, hoping she wasn't making a mistake. "Sarah will be your supervisor. She's waiting to take you on a tour of the building and she'll show you where you'll be working. Sarah answers to Douglas Whitaker."

Susan's green eyes flared with curiosity. "I thought you owned the company."

"I've decided to step down from my position. Douglas will be taking over."

"Too much to handle?"

Kelsey was surprised by the direct question. She had the eerie feeling Susan knew more about her than she was saying. "No, ma'am. I've handled things just fine. But my job here is done."

Susan smiled and stood. "You're absolutely right. I look forward to working for your company. I have a feeling you have some wonderful things in store for it." She paused as she walked to the door. Looking back at Kelsey, she said, "I can see why Ellie Whitaker loves you so much."

Startled, Kelsey groped for a reply. How the hell did Jordan's mom know Ellie?

"Susan, wait," she began, but her new employee was already out the door and Kelsey could hear her speaking to Sarah.

She didn't interrupt. As they walked past her office, Susan cast a brilliant smile in her direction and Kelsey knew she'd made a good choice. Jordan was lucky to have a mother in her life, especially one so full of spunk. Kelsey couldn't help thinking of her own mother and all they could be sharing, especially now. With her role in the business changing, she would have time for the ordinary pleasures of life. She wished she could just sit down and talk with her mother. She missed her badly.

❖

Kelsey only worked for a few more hours. Douglas had everything under control and had ordered her out of the building when she kept interrupting him. Smiling at the thought of her new freedom, she turned onto her street and gasped when she saw Jordan's car. She had the urge to floor the gas pedal and speed right past her, but sooner or later she'd have to face her. She stopped in the driveway and entered the new code. A figure passed the back of her car as the gate opened. *Get your claws out, baby. Here comes the next round.*

Jordan stepped up to her window. "Who the hell do you think you are?"

Kelsey looked straight ahead, avoiding her hypnotic gaze. "I'd like to think I'm Sharon Stone, but I'm really Kelsey Billings."

"Don't play smart-ass with me."

Kelsey gritted her teeth so tight she feared they might crack. "I would never dream of playing anything with you." She stomped the gas and spun her tires as she entered the courtyard. The gate closed, but Jordan was pounding up her driveway.

"You do know you're on private property, don't you?" Kelsey said, getting out of the car. "You know how fast the cops get to my house."

"You're a heartless bitch." Jordan stalked after her as she hurried up the porch steps. "And now you're trying to buy my mother. Will you stop at nothing?"

"How is hiring your mother being heartless? I saved her from flipping burgers, didn't I?" Kelsey heard the spite in her words and wanted to bite her tongue in two.

"You bitch!" Jordan's face contorted into anger. "Did you honestly think hiring her would make this all better? Did you think you could wiggle back into my good graces?"

Kelsey stared at her, astonished. To think she'd gone to the trouble of hiring Susan Porter to help get her out of the hellhole she lived in, and Jordan had the nerve to complain.

"Do you think I hired your mother because of you? Do I *look* like a woman who could give a shit what you think? Don't flatter yourself into thinking this had a damned thing to do with you." Kelsey crammed the key into the lock and kicked the door open. "It's time for you to leave, Jordan."

Jordan glanced toward the gate, then slowly turned her eyes back on Kelsey. "I don't think so."

Jordan wanted to strangle her, to watch those perky lips beg for mercy. Those lips…God. She'd love to cram her mouth over them. She followed Kelsey into the living room, ignoring her dirty looks and muttered expletives.

Kelsey tossed her briefcase on the floor by the couch. "Go ahead. Say your piece and then get the hell out. Wait." She plopped down on the couch. Sarcasm oozed over every word. "Okay. I'm ready. I always like to be sitting when people go for the jugular. The floor is all yours."

Jordan wasn't sure if she wanted to kill her or fuck her brains out. Kelsey's cleavage peeked from between the folds of her silk shirt, beckoning Jordan to have a taste. Her slender legs looked enticing wrapped inside the slacks that clung to every curve of her fine ass. Jordan had trouble concentrating on what she wanted to say.

"How can you just sit there so smugly while your company is tearing people's lives apart?"

Kelsey merely stared at her. She gave a quick shrug, and Jordan stepped toward her, leaving only a few feet between them.

"I *will* tell you this." Kelsey's face contorted into a defensive glare. "You have no idea what you're talking about. You think it's okay to invade my space and behave like I'm the enemy. Why? Because I succeeded where you failed. I made your mother feel happy and secure. Why couldn't *you* do that?"

Infuriated, Jordan yelled, "She wouldn't let me."

"That's pathetic, and you know it. If she was my mother, I'd have moved her out of the projects before she had time to unpack."

"That's easy for you to say, since you don't have a mother."

"You bitch." Kelsey leapt up and her hand shot out with lightning speed.

Jordan caught her by the wrist before the palm connected with her cheek. Kelsey grabbed a fistful of Jordan's hair, tugging like a wildcat. The pain in Jordan's scalp sent a shock wave between her legs. Even while the nails bit in, she clamped her lips over Kelsey's. A soft cry escaped Kelsey's throat and the grip on Jordan's hair loosened. Kelsey's hands fell and she tugged Jordan's shirt free from her waistband.

"Do you know what a bitch you are?" Jordan tilted Kelsey's head back for full access to her neck. She nipped at the delicate skin. Musky scent sweetened on her tongue.

"And proud of it." Kelsey crammed her hand inside Jordan's shirt and raked her nails down her spine.

When Jordan's head snapped back with the sweet pain, Kelsey took the opportunity to torture her exposed neck with bites and kisses. "Don't you think it's time you stop pointing fingers at everyone else for your problems?" she murmured as she worked her way down toward Jordan's breasts.

A groan rumbled from Jordan's throat. She grabbed the folds of Kelsey's shirt and ripped it open. Pearl buttons pinged off the coffee table. Kelsey's chest heaved, pushing her lace-covered breasts closer. Jordan fingered the delicate white fabric before dragging the bra aside. She tasted a nipple, dragging her fingers over the tanned skin of her chest. Kelsey's accusation drummed in her head. She'd reached the same conclusion, but she didn't want to admit it aloud.

"Why the fuck did you come here?" Kelsey whispered.

Jordan knew the answer. She'd wanted to hurt Kelsey, to see her wallow in pain like her mother had the day she lost her job. At the same time, she wanted to see her writhe with need. Jordan couldn't figure out which role she was playing or why. Was she defending her mother's honor, or was that just an excuse to be here? She felt guilty about wanting to ram her fingers inside Kelsey. Was she trying to punish Kelsey for her own weak will?

She slipped her fingers around the button on Kelsey's slacks and popped them open. The zipper slid down with a growl.

"I came to tell you how much I despise you."

She shoved her hand down past the soaking bush and rammed her fingers deep. Kelsey let out a soft cry that practically drove Jordan out of her mind. Her knees went weak.

"I hate you, too." Kelsey gripped Jordan's shirt with her teeth and pulled back. "Take this fucking thing off."

Jordan rammed deeper, wanting to hear her yowl in pain as well as pleasure.

Kelsey screamed and threw her head back. After a few short pants, she clamped her hand around Jordan's wrist, digging a single finger into her skin, halting her deep thrusts. "Take off your damn clothes. Now."

Jordan tossed her on her back on the couch, flopping down on top of her, hand still buried between her legs. "You're not in control here, Kelsey. I am."

She pumped deeper with every thrust. When Kelsey turned to putty in her hands, she drew back and tugged down the sexy slacks. Kelsey kicked against her, flipped over, and slithered across the couch on her stomach.

"Where the hell do you think you're going?" Jordan grabbed her foot and fell on top of her, pressing her into the couch.

Kelsey's answer was lost in the cushions while Jordan dragged the slacks over that glorious ass and off her body. She removed the shirt and bra with no resistance from Kelsey. Running her fingers along the delicate indentation of her spine, she was filled with emotion. She pushed Kelsey's legs apart and slipped her fingers inside.

Kelsey let out a soft cry that melted her. "Fuck me, Jordan. Please."

The hurting game was over. Kelsey's pleas to be taken over that erotic edge snapped Jordan back into the present, denying her the chance to feed her anger anymore. She pulled her fingers out and rolled Kelsey over. Kelsey's chest heaved, lifting her hardened nipples. Jordan took the dark pebbles into her mouth one at a time, slowly sucking. As she rolled her tongue over each tip, she trailed her fingers along Kelsey's lean stomach, and then between her legs. She was slippery and open, her hips thrusting slightly, signaling her desires.

She arched as Jordan thrust inside, moaning with each stroke. Her hands hooked Jordan's pants and she tore them down urgently. This time Jordan didn't stop her. With her free hand she helped drag the garments off, then gasped when a finger slid over her clit.

"No. Net yet." She wanted to give all her attention to Kelsey.

She placed her thumb on Kelsey's clit and began circling, bringing Kelsey's urgent pants to desperate cries. She could feel

Kelsey's orgasm coiling as she pumped faster and harder. She saw only Kelsey. Nothing existed but the two of them. Kelsey's legs fell apart, no modesty left to her. Jordan rammed her fingers deeper, faster, meeting the rise of her hips, circling her clit with every thrust. The slick inner walls squeezed her fingers as pressure built. Kelsey humped against her with wild, frantic thrusts.

Jordan threw her body against her hand, diving in and out, over and over, until Kelsey went rigid beneath her and tightened her grip on the back of her neck. Her body writhed and convulsed. She screamed out and rocked under Jordan's weight until her hard pumps simmered down to light pulses around Jordan's fingers. When her breathing slowed, she stared up at Jordan and slipped a hand between them, sliding down Jordan's stomach until she found her wet pussy.

A delicate finger slipped across her clit, and within seconds, Jordan was screaming with an orgasm crashing through her. She rocked over Kelsey's hand until her knees were too weak to hold her and she collapsed, snuggling into Kelsey's neck, inhaling their mixed scents. She lay still, listening to Kelsey's heart.

Would she laugh her ass off if I told her I was in love with her?

Chapter Fifteen

Kelsey inhaled Jordan's musky scent deeply. Her eyes fluttered open and her heart twisted in her chest at the feel of Jordan pressed so tightly against her.

This was wrong, two women tearing at each other. She forced herself to stare beyond the dark, silky hair hanging only inches from her face. With every ounce of willpower she could muster, she slid out from under Jordan, away from those strong arms and skilled hands. She picked up her crumpled slacks and quickly tugged them over her hips, then pulled her shirt on, tugging the edges together to cover herself.

Jordan got up from the couch. She was very quiet. Kelsey watched her slide her jeans over her hips. Her insides ached from the orgasm that had raced through her body. Beyond a shadow of a doubt, Jordan was the best lover she'd ever had, the first lover she'd ever truly loved.

"Look at us." Kelsey lifted her arm to see the light finger bruises darkening her wrists. Her hair hung in pale tangles around her face. "We act like we despise each other."

Jordan brushed her palms against her forehead. "I'll never understand you or your company. I'm not sure I want to. But we have a connection."

Kelsey almost forgot to breathe. She waited, wanting to hear from Jordan's lips what she knew in her heart. When Jordan was silent, she swallowed back the impulse to go to her and run her fingers through her hair, to kiss the lips she dreamed about. She bit back the tears threatening to overflow her lids and turned away. Jordan wasn't going to say it.

Kelsey wanted to be alone, to curl into a ball and let the tears flow. She would not be weak in front of this strong woman. She wouldn't show defeat to anyone. She walked to the door and gripped the knob. Staring down at her white knuckles, she said, "You can find your way out."

"Wait."

Jordan's sharp cry forced Kelsey around to face her. The expression on her face made Kelsey's legs unsteady. She sucked in a breath, letting it slowly escape as Jordan walked toward her.

"I can't do this," Jordan said.

Kelsey felt a dark wave of disappointment crash over her. "I won't apologize for anything I've done in my life," she said coldly. "I am who I am. I'm proud of that person. And you'll never know the real me."

Jordan reared back as though she'd been struck. "Do you know the real you? Do you know what you want?"

"Yes. Do you?"

Jordan's eyes softened. She touched Kelsey's arm. "I think I do, but I want to ask something of you."

Kelsey's heart started hammering again. "Yes?"

"I need to take a few days alone to think about everything. My mom. My work. Us."

Us. Kelsey struggled not to fall into Jordan's arms and beg her to stay and never leave. "Is there an 'us'?" she asked, afraid to hear the answer.

Jordan's warm lips pressed against her forehead. "For me there is."

Hot tears clouded Kelsey's vision. She leaned into Jordan so that she wouldn't sink to the floor. The need to hold her was more than Kelsey could handle. She slid her arms around that athletic waist and sighed as Jordan's tight stomach pressed against hers.

"For me, too," she said, close to Jordan's ear.

"Then let's not throw this away."

"Okay." Kelsey wanted to say more, but she sensed that Jordan was taking a big step. She had to let her make the next move in her own time.

Wild joy rocked through her and she couldn't stop smiling. Jordan had feelings for her, and she hadn't even found out about the plan for Billings Industries yet.

Jordan stared at her as if she were seeing her for the first time. "I have to go."

Kelsey nodded. She chewed on her bottom lip, fighting back tears. "I'll be here when you get back."

Jordan smiled. "That means a lot."

She kissed Kelsey again, tenderly on the lips, and walked away.

Kelsey watched the love of her life from the window. "Please come back to me," she whispered.

❖

"I'm so excited to be moving." Susan Porter carried a box to the front door and then retuned to the tiny kitchen.

"I wish you would let me carry those," Jordan said.

"You're doing enough. You're supposed to be in Palm Springs, taking time out."

"I could have been if you'd waited another week." She still couldn't believe it. Her mom had found the new condominium within twenty-four hours. "Hell, you haven't even started your job yet."

"I'm being efficient," her mom said, obviously pleased with herself. "I won't have time to move once I'm working again. Besides, I thought you wanted me out of the projects."

"I do, but—"

"You're upset that I'm working for the enemy."

"That's not it at all," Jordan bit back.

"Really? Would you like to talk about it?"

"No."

"You sure don't sound happy."

Jordan picked up an empty box and started placing porcelain knickknacks inside. "How can you work for her?" she blurted before she could silence herself.

It was two days since she'd seen Kelsey and she still hadn't settled on a course of action. Her life was heading uphill. She just prayed she didn't do something stupid and tumble down the other side. She loved Kelsey and she wanted to find a way to get past all the hurt. But Kelsey was content in her multi-million-dollar empire and said she would not apologize for anything. Jordan didn't know how they were going to find common ground.

"Work for who, honey?" her mother asked.

Jordan rolled her eyes. "You know very well who I'm talking about."

"I work for a *him*. Not a *her.*"

"What happened to Kelsey?" Jordan tried to sound uncaring.

"You wouldn't believe me if I told you. You listen with your ears and not your heart."

"What the hell is that supposed to mean?"

Her mother constructed another box. The screech of the tape dispenser set Jordan's nerves on edge.

"That woman worked her ass off doing what was expected of her." Susan yanked a mug from Jordan's hand and shoved it in the box. "One day, when you grow up, you'll understand that everything isn't always as it seems."

"I don't want to discuss Kelsey Billings today, if that's okay with you."

He mother snorted. "You never could admit when you were wrong. That's your problem. You're stubborn."

"Oh, I wonder where I get *that* from." Jordan swung a couple of boxes into her arms and stalked out of the kitchen.

"Kelsey's far from an enemy. She's a broken angel." A female voice came from behind her.

Jordan whipped around to face a silver-haired woman. Navy cotton pants fit snugly around her handlebar hips and her motherly shape filled out a flower-print blouse. Her hair was pulled into a clip at the back of her head.

"Hi, Ellie. Thanks for coming over." Susan looked delighted. "This is my daughter. Jordan, you've already met Ellie's husband, Artie Whitaker."

"Yes, I remember." Jordan gave a polite nod. "It's nice to meet you, Ellie."

"Likewise."

Jordan studied the older women. Their silly smiles seemed to be at her expense. Puzzled, she asked, "How do you two know each other?"

"Art class," Ellie said.

"Aerobics," Susan chimed in.

Both women started giggling like schoolchildren.

"I think we should sit down," Ellie peered around. "Is there any furniture left?"

"All of it," Susan said happily. "I decided to splash out. They're delivering my new sofa set to the condo tomorrow."

"You didn't tell me about that," Jordan sputtered. "Have you blown what was left of your savings?"

Ellie raised her eyebrows. "I think I now know why Kelsey has been wringing her hands over you."

She parked herself on the couch, while Susan poured glasses of tea.

"Tell her," came the instruction from the kitchen.

Ellie stopped cackling and pasted a serious expression on her face. "Your mother thinks it's time you learned the truth, Jordan. But she says you won't listen to her."

"It depends what she's saying," Jordan mumbled.

Ellie's eyes blazed with determination. "I love Kelsey and I won't allow you to hurt her."

Jordan had to close her lips firmly together. Controlling her tone, she said, "I think Kelsey can take care of herself."

"You seem to have a very low opinion of her."

"I've been trying to see past her unethical business practices."

"That's big of you." Accepting her iced tea from Susan, Ellie asked, "Is she always like this?"

"Always."

"Thanks a lot, Mom." Jordan sipped her tea.

"Have you ever loved someone so much that you'd fight to the death to protect them?" Ellie asked.

Jordan's heart fluttered as Kelsey's face oozed into her memory. Slowly, she said, "I can understand that feeling."

"Well, Artie and I love that child just as if she's our very own. That's why I looked for your mom after Artie told me about meeting you. He could see there was trouble between you and Kelsey. I wanted to help."

Jordan frowned at her mother. "So you've been talking about me behind my back and trying to interfere in my personal life."

Susan nodded unapologetically. "That's what moms do."

Jordan sat down, resigning herself. The sooner she heard what her mom's new best friend had to say, the sooner she could finish packing boxes and get out of here. She was also curious. If Kelsey had close friends who would defend her as fiercely as the people Jordan had met so far, there was more to her than the corporate villain Jordan loved to hate. She already knew that, but she felt compelled to know more.

"Okay, I'm listening," she said.

"Kelsey's grandfather was an alcoholic. His dream in life was to own his own business. He tried but he bankrupted. From that moment, he turned sour, blaming his family and friends for his downfall instead of pointing the finger at himself. He beat Kelsey's father, and the rest of the family, on a regular basis."

Ellie paused to wipe away her tears. "He turned those boys into thieves and beggars. John grew up never knowing what it was about owning a business that would turn a man into a monster, but he didn't want other families to go through what he went through."

"That's ironic," Jordan remarked. "When you consider how many people have been laid off because of him."

Ellie sighed. "That was never what he wanted. He started Billings Industries to save business owners and their families from a life of hell. He wanted to help by buying companies that were going under. I'm not sure why it all went wrong."

"Greed?" Jordan suggested.

Ellie met her eyes, refusing to be goaded. "Kelsey just put my son in charge of the company and he has the job of implementing a new plan."

"I'll be involved," Susan said excitedly. "Kelsey told me about it. The company is going to invest in turning businesses around and keeping people in their jobs."

Jordan shifted in her seat, a nervous knot twisting her gut. Heaviness, sick and cloying, spread through her. "A new plan?"

"She and Douglas have been working on it for months," Ellie said. "She always hated what the company had become but she couldn't tell her father that. She didn't want to hurt him."

Jordan fought to untangle her muddled thoughts. "If she's not running the company anymore, what's she doing?"

Ellie looked her in the eye. "I think that depends on you."

❖

Kelsey rolled a suitcase into her dressing room. Darren was inspecting his face in the mirror. He claimed her makeup light was more flattering than his.

"Honey? Um, I didn't pack," he said, as she unzipped the bag in front of the closet. "If we're leaving today for Hawaii, I need to go do that."

She chuckled. "Not Hawaii. I'm quitting."

"You're not serious." He lowered his mascara wand. "This place would be nothing without you. I mean, I know you could care less about money, but some of us rather like it."

Kelsey tossed miniskirts and halter tops into the bag. When the last costume garment was pulled from its hanger, she noticed a business suit crumpled in the corner on the floor.

"My whole life has been spent behind a fake smile and hardened heart," she said, gathering the designer jacket and pants. "This place was my hideaway. It was a change, something different. Being here, I could hide the person I didn't want anyone to see. But the dancer isn't the real me."

"Of course not." Darren smiled. "Ask any stripper."

"I'm not going to be either one of those people anymore," she said.

Darren's lips quivered. "Oh, honey. You're in love." He threw his arms around her and squished her face against his chest. "Isn't it the most beautiful feeling in the world?"

Kelsey felt the sting of her tears but held them back. Someone cleared their throat behind them. Sharon moved into the room.

"Is everything okay?"

"It will be." Kelsey's anger spiked instantly. Sharon looked so innocent.

"Did you get any leads on the person who trashed your house?"

"No. Did you get a kick out of paying Paula to get a lap dance?"

Sharon's guilty hesitation spoke volumes. "Shit. I'm sorry. That was very stupid of me."

"I'd say so. What were you thinking?"

Sharon's hard glare met hers. "I wanted that woman away from you. I thought if I got rid of her, I could have you back."

"You never had me, Sharon. I never promised you love. What we had was fun, but that's all it ever was."

"I know. I'm sorry, Kelsey."

"And the death threats. You're behind them, aren't you? Just another sick ploy to get me back?"

Sharon gasped. "I would never do that. I might love you, but I'm not a moron."

Kelsey stared, trying to read her. For some reason, her inner warning system had poofed out the day she met Jordan.

Sharon grabbed her hands. "Whoever is doing this to you means business, Kelsey. I'm really worried about you."

If she was lying, she was doing a hell of a job. Confusion clouded Kelsey's mind. If the stalker wasn't Sharon, then it had to be Paula. But Paula had seemed okay about the past the last time they spoke.

"What are you doing?" Sharon stared down at the suitcase.

"You'll need to find another dancer," Kelsey said. "I'm not coming back."

❖

"What happened to Kelsey's mother?" Jordan asked as they finishing packing the last few boxes.

Ellie turned tear-filled blue eyes on her. "She gave up. I think she would have taken the kids with her, but she couldn't bear to hurt John. She meant the world to Kelsey. So did John. She's been nursing a broken heart. Until you came along."

Jordan could only stare, too numb to say a word.

"And you, you stubborn ass, let her down," her mother said.

Jordan felt a bite of betrayal. "I was defending you."

"I don't need defending. I needed my ass kicked for brooding instead of getting a job."

Jordan shook her head. She couldn't believe what she was hearing. She didn't give a shit how much of a horrible life Kelsey might had lived, what demons she had, or who she'd lost, she was still a person who tossed people out on their asses and made a fortune from it.

"You're my mother," she said. "I had to defend you."

Something must have hit home with her mom. Instead of throwing one of her usual comebacks, she leaned over to hug her. "I'm sorry. I should be thankful my daughter cares. But don't you dare blame someone else for all our problems."

Her words dispelled the last bit of Jordan's anger. That's exactly what Kelsey's grandfather had done. He'd blamed everyone else for his downfall instead of blaming himself. Jordan realized she was no different. It was easier to blame Kelsey than admit that she couldn't resolve her mother's difficulties herself. How stupid could she have been? She'd almost lost the only lover she'd ever cared deeply about because she was too stubborn to face the truth.

And the truth was very simple: she couldn't live another day without Kelsey.

"I think you've heard enough to know what kind of person Kelsey is," Ellie said. "But in case you need more evidence, read this." She dropped a newspaper clipping on Jordan's lap.

Kelsey Billings is the founder of New Hope, an organization aimed at saving businesses from bankruptcy. Ms. Billings is well known for her philanthropic support of Los Angeles charities, and recently donated a million dollars to assist mothers and children fleeing domestic violence. Her initiative, the New Beginnings program, provides housing and educational assistance to victims of abuse. All construction was paid for by the John Billings Sr. Foundation, named for Ms. Billings's grandfather. Ms. Billings is also the founder of New Generations, an organization involved in finding missing persons.

Jordan thought about Kelsey's mother. Kelsey hadn't sat back and let her sorrows control her life. She was doing something for the future since there wasn't a damn thing she could do about the past. This woman wasn't just a broken angel, she had a broken soul and she was trying to repair the damage alone. It was time for Jordan to find her and offer to share that task.

"I'm in love with an angel," she whispered.

"Oh, I almost forgot." Ellie held out a yellow envelope. "Paula Riching dropped this off earlier, asked me to deliver it to Kelsey. I think I'll let you do the honors." She picked up a roll of tape. "Susan, did I tell you about the lovely new addition to my house? Paula built it. She has her own construction company."

Jordan couldn't help but catch the insinuation. It was obvious that Ellie knew nothing about Paula's hostility to Kelsey and was trying to imply that if Jordan didn't play her cards right, Kelsey had other options.

She opened the envelope and unfolded the note inside. At first she couldn't comprehend what she was looking at. A funeral notice was stapled to the page. She read the name "George Paul Riching" and instantly lowered her eyes to the words printed beneath the clipping:

> YOU KILLED MY FATHER, YOU WICKED WHORE.
> I'M COMING TO GET YOU.

Fear, thick and cloying, clawed through Jordan's heart. She bolted off the couch.

"Get the cops to Kelsey's house! Now!"

The papers fluttered to the floor as she tore out of the apartment.

CHAPTER SIXTEEN

Kelsey wiped tears from her face with a tissue and flipped to the next page in her the photo album. Her mother, a bright smile stretched across her gorgeous face, looked adoringly at her father. Her father, tall and proud, stared back at her like there wasn't another woman in the world. He had eyes only for her.

Kelsey would never forget his love. She'd give anything to have him back right now, to hear him tell her one more time how proud he was of her. And Kevin, even the loser that he was, would get just as much attention. Her father had never missed a single day, telling each of them how much he loved and cherished them. She let loose a sob. In two weeks, she'd be facing the anniversary of his death. How could her mother and brother have left her to deal with everything, alone and falling apart? Running the business had made her a hard-ass bitch 24/7. Becoming a dancer had made her a seductive goddess. And now, she wasn't either of those things. She was just Kelsey Billings, owner of a company that would be doing what it was meant to do from the start.

Swamped in her memories, she lovingly ran her finger over the photo, along her father's squared chin. "Here's to you, Daddy. Like father, like daughter."

Except that Kelsey didn't plan to lose her love because she couldn't make changes in her life. She curled into a ball on the couch, wondering when she would hear from Jordan. The thought of holding her again was all that had kept her going for the past two days.

A dog barked in the distance, drawing her attention to the window. She pushed the photo album away and rose. In the early evening light, it was hard to make out the shadows around her yard. She couldn't see anyone, yet she could feel something…or someone. She went to the front door to check that it was locked. And then she heard it. Footsteps on the porch. Too light to be a man, but too heavy to be an animal. Fear gripped her heart.

"Who's there?" she called through the heavy wood.

"It's me, Paula, your new neighbor."

Kelsey kept the chain on as she opened the door. "You should have phoned."

Paula waved a bottle of wine above her head. "I came bearing gifts."

"How did you get in the gate?" Kelsey felt foolish for her paranoia, but if Paula could get in so could anyone.

Paula shrugged. "I work in the construction business. Ever heard of ladders?"

"You jumped over?"

Paula shrugged. "I wanted to surprise you. Not in a bad way."

She stared at the chain. Embarrassed by her unwelcoming behavior, Kelsey hurried to let her in. She was thankful for the company and she wanted to put the past behind them. Paula had seemed to want that when they had lunch together.

Paula walked through, a wide smile on her face.

"What? No dinner?" Kelsey teased. "I thought new neighbors were supposed to bring potluck or something."

"I'm not good in the kitchen." Paula handed her the wine and looked around as Kelsey closed the door. "Nice place."

"Come sit down." Kelsey led her to the living room and Paula flopped onto the couch.

She pulled the photo album into her lap immediately, and

started turning pages. Kelsey found some wineglasses and slid onto the other end of the couch.

"That was my father." She pointed to a photo. "You and I have a lot in common. We both had great dads and miss them terribly."

Paula turned a curious stare on her, as though rummaging Kelsey's face for an underlying meaning. She closed the album and laid it aside. "I'm curious. Did you or your dad shed a tear when you killed my father?"

Kelsey sat frozen to her spot, panic eating through her gut. She shook her head, and let her gaze travel around her, looking for something to defend herself with. Taking her eyes off her opponent—something she knew better than to do—proved a stupid act. Paula was on her before she could blink, straddling her stomach, fingers wrapped around her neck, squeezing her throat.

"My dad mourned himself right into the grave because of your father." Paula bared her teeth while her grip tightened. "He called himself a failure."

Kelsey grabbed at the fingers choking her. She kicked her legs into thin air, her lungs burning with need. Suddenly Paula released her grip and climbed off her as calmly as she would dismount a horse. Kelsey slid off the couch onto the floor, coughing and gagging. Holding her throat, she watched Paula closely.

"Did you honestly think I would let you get away with what you and your father did to him?" Paula's lips glistened with drool.

"But you said we should move on."

Paula dropped to the floor in front of her, glaring like a maniac. "I lie good, you pathetic whore."

Kelsey stiffened, unable to take her eyes off the evil before her. She backed up until the coffee table halted her. Paula rose and stood over her.

"Poor little Kelsey. *Oh no*, her daddy died. Let's feel sorry for her. *Oh no*, Mommy ran away. Let's feel sorry for Kelsey even more. *Poor Kelsey.*" She rubbed her bloodshot eyes. "Did anyone ever pity *my* father? Did anyone ever wonder why *he* gave up?"

Anger replaced Kelsey's fear. She tightened her hands into fists, matched Paula's glare, and levered herself up from the floor. She'd be damned if Paula was going to make a mockery of her.

"You don't know a damn thing about me or my family, or my life. Don't you dare taint my father's name by letting it roll off that filthy tongue. You're pathetic."

"You think you have everyone fooled." Spittle flew from Paula's mouth. "Ellie and Artie are blind to your faults. Must be fucking nice to hand over thousands of dollars to charity like it's pennies in a wishing well. My father groveled for every dime."

"Did it ever cross your mind that your father was the one who bankrupted his business, not us?" Kelsey hissed.

But Paula wasn't done ranting. "When in the hell is everyone going to stop feeling sorry for a stripper and her worthless, piece-of-shit father who drove a good man to his death?"

Kelsey felt strong. She'd done everything within her power to right the wrongs left by her family. The slate was clean now.

"I want you to leave," she said calmly.

Paula blinked hard, and then dove for her. They fell back onto the carpet, twisting and turning, yanking and pulling at each other's hair. Kelsey felt herself leap effortlessly into fight mode. All her years of training crashed through her mind. Paula was a larger, stronger opponent, but she was angry and clumsy. Kelsey gritted her teeth and jabbed her elbow into Paula's nose. When Paula covered her face, she jabbed again, and again, and again, then grabbed Paula's short hair and rammed her face into the floor.

"We did not kill your father. He worked himself to the grave. Which is why...my father...bought him out. How dare you blame us."

Kelsey wanted to say more, to scream that her own father

also drove himself to his own grave, but she knew it was useless. Paula needed to blame someone else. She pounded Paula's face to the floor one more time, then pushed away and charged for the phone. As she grabbed the receiver, a sharp, burning pain scored down her back. She screamed and fell to her knees.

Paula dove on top of her, flattening her against the carpet. She slammed Kelsey's head onto the floor, bellowing crazed insults. Stars brightened behind Kelsey's eyelids. Pain sheared through her head.

"Your hands are bloody with his death, and it's time to answer for your crime."

Something stung with ferocity and dug deeper into Kelsey's back. She looked up into eyes filled with pure evil. "Paula, please stop. I know how terrible it was to suffer your loss."

"You fucking cunt. Don't think you can sympathize with me. You and your father took away the only thing in my life I cared about."

Kelsey curled her legs under Paula's chest and shoved. Paula flew off her and sprawled on her back. When Kelsey tried to stand her knees went weak. Her vision blurred, then cleared. Her arms tingled and her face felt like it was on fire. Her heart slowed to a crawl in her chest. Paula watched her placidly, making no effort to seize her again.

"You should have seen the look on your daddy's face when I showed up at his office with a gun and told him how his little whore would die a slow, agonizing death. I guess his poor old heart just couldn't take it." She laughed evilly. "It was so fucking sweet how he grasped his chest, crawling across the floor on his hands and knees, begging me not to hurt you."

Tears welled in Kelsey's eyes as she visualized her father begging for her life and not his own. It tore her heart in half to think he'd died in fear. Anger bubbled into pure hatred. Her vision blurred again, and her body refused to obey her demand to move. She tried to crawl toward Paula, determined to squeeze the last breath from her lungs, to avenge his death. Her arms buckled, spilling her onto the carpet. She gasped for breath. When her vision cleared, she saw the tip of a syringe close to her body. Fear ran the length of her while her nerve endings tingled.

"Today, Kelsey, is the day you die. I thought it fitting to do it on the anniversary of my daddy's death." Paula wiped blood from her lips and grinned. "When they find you, you'll be pumped full of drugs, lying beside your father's grave. Your suicide letter is rather sweet, explaining how you couldn't live with my dad's death on your conscience. God knows, you went on with life like he never existed, like none of us ever existed, you fucking slut."

She grabbed one of Kelsey's arms and started dragging her across the carpet. Kelsey tried to scream but her body wasn't hers anymore. She tried to reach out and grab Paula's leg, but her arms were frozen. The room spun faster and faster. Blue lights beaconed across the walls.

Paula dropped her arm and moved away from her. "Fuck, Artie is going to make me do this the hard way."

Kelsey's world spun one final loop, and then her eyes closed. *I'm sorry, Daddy.*

Blackness consumed her.

❖

Love, adrenaline, and the most gut-wrenching fear Jordan had ever known pushed her foot harder on the accelerator. She took every twist and turn at race speed, praying she wasn't too late. By the time she turned onto Kelsey's road, she was begging God to keep her safe.

The squealing of tires dragged her away from her thoughts. Police cars flew past her, joining several that already lined the street ahead. The police had opened the gate to Kelsey's house. Jordan pulled over, not wanting to draw attention to herself. She locked the Viper and ran to a house two doors down from Kelsey's, where the front yard was open to the street.

Without hesitation, she bolted behind the large Victorian-style home. A dog flew against the porch door and security lights bathed the yard. Jordan scaled the wall to the next property. Trees hung over the yard like a green awning. Moss hung from their branches, giving an eerie feeling to the pitch-black night. The house seemed empty. The owners were probably away.

Jordan caught her breath. She could hear the police out on the street. One of them yelled for Paula to come out. Something stirred and Jordan slipped behind a tree. The glow of the moon slivered between the branches and cast a silhouette into relief. Paula was on the wall between the two properties. She had Kelsey slung over her shoulder. She couldn't make the jump, weighed down, so she dropped Kelsey first, then sprang after her.

Jordan had to act now or Kelsey would be dead, if she wasn't already. She ducked behind a bush, trying to get a better look at the beauty lying lifeless on the ground. She couldn't make out breathing, twitching, anything. *Dear God, don't let it end like this. Don't let me be too late.*

With fear and love working magic, she stepped from behind the bush, rising to her full height. "What the fuck are you doing?"

Paula whipped around, eyes full of evil. "Back off!"

Kelsey didn't flinch, which made Jordan sick to her stomach. She wanted just a shred of evidence she was alive. Her blond hair was fanned out around her head, her lips were the color of death.

"It's over, Paula. The cops have this place surrounded." If she begged, would it work? Would Paula be afraid enough of being arrested to spare Kelsey? "Just run. You have time. Don't hurt her."

Paula answered with hard, gushing whoops of laughter. She dropped to her knees and pressed a syringe against Kelsey's neck.

A roar of hatred blasted through Jordan. She wanted her hands on the bitch who'd dared cause Kelsey harm. She wanted to hear her begging for mercy. She ground her teeth together and balled her hands into fists to keep from diving on her, fearing the split-second needle jab into that precious throat.

"You're funny." Paula slid her hand over her stomach, massaging as if the effort of laughing had caused physical pain. "I'd willingly walk into a gas chamber just to see this bitch dead."

Jordan stood frozen, not sure whether to pounce or run like hell. Driven by instinct alone, she demanded, "Where were you when your father's business was sinking?"

Paula shot to her feet, the reaction Jordan had hoped for. She needed to redirect Paula's rage. She could hear voices. The police were moving in behind Kelsey's house. Before long they would fan out to the neighboring properties. All she had to do was buy time.

"Why didn't you save his business?" she asked.

Paula bared her teeth. "He wouldn't let me."

Jordan knew her type—the ones that blamed everyone else for their failures and inadequacies, just like she'd done. She wanted to get her farther away from Kelsey—close enough to strike.

"Why? Because you're a female? Women can't work in a man's world, right? Old-fashioned daddy wouldn't let his precious little girl take control? Is that why you're jealous of Kelsey, because her daddy believed in her?"

"Fuck you!" Paula took a menacing step toward her.

It was the only chance Jordan might get. She charged. Paula skirted to the side. Jordan skidded, turned, and back-kicked the syringe from her hand. Paula's eyes widened as her gaze targeted the needle. Jordan caught sight of the white cylinder and charged for it. Paula raced after her, clawing at her shirt.

Jordan stomped the needle. Her shirt was released. Paula was racing away from her.

"There they are," an officer yelled from the top of the wall.

Jordan raced to Kelsey, dropped down beside her, and felt for a pulse. "She's alive," she yelled to the cop. "Hurry."

Anger and adrenaline set her feet in motion. She sprinted across the open yard and hoisted herself over the fence to the next property. She ran, twisting in and out of trees, closing in on the blond head ten feet in front of her. Her leg and arm muscles screamed in protest, coiling and bunching as she pumped them faster and faster. Her breaths were gasps as she sucked in air. She braced herself to climb the next wall, when Paula stopped suddenly and turned toward her. She crouched into a defensive posture, arms stretched out in front of her, hands poised into fists.

Jordan knew she was going to get her last competition. And what a sweet ass-whooping it would be. Smiling, she locked her gaze on the bitch.

"I must warn you, I know how to fight." Paula gave her a defiant nod, as if Jordan should tremble.

"Good. Kicking your ass will be a pleasure." Jordan crouched and the circling began.

Paula took a soft jab at her, testing the waters. Jordan jerked her head back, keeping her arms close to her body. Paula took another jab, this time meaning harm. Jordan jumped to the side and rammed her fist into Paula's rib cage. A grunt of air whooshed from her mouth.

"That slut ain't worth fighting for," Paula snarled and circled.

Jordan's grin was full of malice. "She's well worth the ass-kicking you're about to get."

Paula jabbed at her. Jordan ducked; this time she uppercut into the bitch's stomach. Paula fell, rolled, and popped right back up on her feet.

"She's a whore," Paula taunted.

"It's not her fault your father died." Jordan tempted her closer by backing up a step, careful to watch her every move. "Instead of being a coward, you should have stood up to him."

Paula's mouth flew open in outrage. Jordan jabbed, catching her square in the nose. Her head jolted back with the force. As if unharmed, she dropped to the ground and kicked Jordan's feet out from under her. The move was one Jordan hadn't completely expected, suggesting her opponent had some general martial arts training. But Paula was a bully. She wasn't the kind of fighter to exercise patience or restraint. Jordan knew she had her beat. She only hoped the police wouldn't catch up to them too soon. She wanted enough time to pile on the damage before they hauled Paula's ass off to the crazy house.

"After I get done with you, that whore is mine," Paula was stupid enough to announce.

Possessiveness and keen instinct took over. An image of Kelsey flipped through Jordan's mind. This woman didn't know her angel very well. And Jordan was tired of playing games. It was time to put this bitch down and get back to the love of her life. She had some making up to do.

She dipped to the side and gave a wide round-kick, catching Paula in the mouth. Paula groaned and lifted a hand to her bloody lips.

"Freeze!" a cop bellowed.

Jordan thought she recognized Artie, his voice heavy with adrenaline and exasperation. She didn't dare glance over her shoulder—didn't dare take her eyes off her opponent. She heard a scream. Kelsey. The sound was sweet music to her ears. For a split second, Paula didn't exist. The world revolved around the beauty waiting for her.

"Why are you fighting for that whore?" Paula spat some blood and Jordan glimpsed the face of insanity—a woman truly on the verge of visiting la-la land.

She lowered her hands to her side.

Paula stared in confusion and then an evil smile spread over her features. She jabbed. With lightning speed, Jordan dropped to the ground, rolled, popped up behind her, and shoved her forward with every ounce of strength she had. Without waiting for her to fall, she was already diving on her.

Paula bucked beneath her and rolled over. Jordan straddled her and drove her fists into her face, one punch after the next, pummeling her. She wanted to see blood ooze from the woman who'd made her baby's life hell for months and who had tried to take her life tonight. In her blind rage, she meant to beat Paula to death, to watch the last breath gasp from her chest, but rough hands grabbed her on either side and dragged her off.

An officer went down beside Paula and handcuffed her.

"Kelsey?" Jordan turned to Artie.

"She's all right. Thanks to you." He pointed toward the street, and Jordan ran with every ounce of energy she had left in her body.

Kelsey was leaning against Artie's cruiser, looking as if she could barely hold herself upright. Jordan noticed for the first time how many cars were around them, flashing blue and white lights. She couldn't reach Kelsey fast enough. What felt like miles were only yards—the longest yards of her life. As she neared the car, Kelsey all but dove into her arms.

The feel of her slender body, the smell of her jasmine hair, and the sound of her sobs, crushed Jordan's heart. It terrified her to realize that the woman she was desperately in love with could have died at the hands of a lunatic. She feathered Kelsey's face with her lips, brushing her hair back to see those mesmerizing blue eyes.

"I was so scared," Kelsey mumbled, hugging Jordan with quivering arms. "She drugged me."

"You're okay now." Jordan pulled her closer, taking the weight from Kelsey's trembling legs. She wanted to lift her into her arms and tote her all the way back home.

Kelsey stared up at her, tears staining her flushed cheeks. "I was scared for you." She gave Jordan's arm a soft jab, still full of spunk even if the drugs were apparent in her speech and motor skills. "She killed my father,"

"She's insane, baby."

Footsteps called their attention. Paula glared at them from between two officers. Her deranged stare fell on Kelsey and a wicked, teeth-baring smile contorted her blood-covered face.

"I'll be back to get you, Kelsey." She puckered her bloodstained lips and blew a kiss.

"You killed my daddy!" Kelsey lunged unsteadily for her, but Jordan held her back.

Paula grinned. "I wish. Sorry to say I only helped the process." Her gaze whipped to Jordan. "I'll be back for you, too, bitch."

Jordan longed to snap her neck in half so Kelsey would never live another day in fear. She returned her nasty grin. "It'll be my pleasure to finish what I started."

Paula's smile vanished. She took one last look at Kelsey before the officer yanked her forward.

As Artie escorted them back to Kelsey's house, Kelsey was very quiet in Jordan's arms. The drug that had immobilized her was wearing off but she couldn't walk. Jordan wanted to ask her if she was okay, but she sensed a need within her for silence. She shared the feeling, so she gave her breathing room and concentrated on what she wanted to say to her.

She started with a whisper against the soft blond hair. "I love you."

Kelsey tilted her head back and smiled.

Even though her body was still quivering, Kelsey could feel her energy gathering.

"We need to take care of a few more details before we leave," the paramedic said. "The drug is usually out of the system within twelve hours, but there could still be some side effects."

"You shouldn't wait to go to the hospital," Jordan said.

Kelsey shook her head. "I want to be at home."

She'd been poked and probed enough, and she was starting to feel like her old self again. Her energy was coming back, along with anger and her newfound love.

Fear came and went in waves. What if Jordan hadn't come? What if Paula had been armed with more than a syringe full of drugs? If she'd had a gun, she could easily have killed Jordan. She was insane, and once she made that comment about her father, Kelsey had been certain she wouldn't make it out alive. She hated herself for trusting her. Where had her instincts vanished to? She was trained to read people. Why hadn't she read Paula?

Love? Had love interfered?

Artie shook hands with the paramedic, and Kelsey followed them onto the porch. She wrapped her arms around Artie's neck. "Thank you for always being there."

"I couldn't imagine being anywhere else in the world." His eyes filled with tears. "Now, go get some rest. You gave us all a scare and Ellie's going to expect a visit tomorrow. She's been worried out of her mind." He stepped off the porch, then turned back around. "Oh, yeah. Make sure you get hold of Sharon and that goofball you call your best friend. They've had me on the cell phone every five minutes."

Sharon. Kelsey felt sick with remorse. She'd all but accused her of being the stalker. Would she still want a friendship? Was that possible if love wasn't involved?

And just like that, Kelsey knew her life was going to start anew with the morning light. There would be no more mourning the ones that had left her. Her father's dreams were but a memory now—her grandfather's legacy a foundation she could use to support the dreams of others. Sweet freedom swirled around her. She felt like a brand new person. With a smile, she released pain from her heart and turned around.

Jordan was standing right behind her.

Kelsey met her "need you" gaze. Love, strong and powerful, snagged its talons through her heart. The love of her life, the savior of the day, her protector, stood before her, love flowing all around her—for Kelsey. There was no more guessing. No more worrying about the what-ifs. Gentle, loving arms wrapped around her and Jordan led her inside the house.

She closed the door and punched the button to close the gate. "No more interruptions tonight."

Kelsey took her hand and started across the carpet, wanting nothing more than to be naked in her strong arms.

Jordan drew back, halting her progress. "We need to talk."

Kelsey's heart leapt into her throat. Jordan wanted to *know* about her life. And Kelsey wanted to tell her. But what mattered most was that Jordan loved her even before she said another word. She had already decided to take Kelsey just as she was.

"Are you sure?" Kelsey asked.

Jordan smiled. "Of course I'm sure. I love you."

Pure joy rolled through Kelsey, washing away all that had gone before. "I love you, too."

"I want to know everything…anything," Jordan said.

Kelsey crept into her arms. She ran a finger along the ridge of her lips. "Anything?"

"Anything."

"It's a deal. But first," Kelsey pressed her lips to Jordan's ear, "I dare you to make love to me."

About the Author

Larkin lives in a "blink and you've missed it" town on the East Coast with her partner of thirteen years, a portion of their seven bratty children, and a Chunky Punk grandson who adores his Nana. She was recently blessed with another grandson who has the cutest smile you've ever seen.

The journey of writing wasn't in Larkin's cards many moons ago. She hated school and thought English teachers were the devil. When the voices in her head screamed louder than her children, she ruled out multiple personalities and let the writing begin.

I'll be damned if a novel wasn't born...more tumbling out behind that one.

Let the voices continue. Let the clatter of keys continue. Let the birth of erotic creations continue.

And may you all be there to be captivated by them all.

Happy Reading,
Larkin

Books Available From Bold Strokes Books

Lake Effect Snow by C.P. Rowlands. News correspondent Annie T. Booker and FBI Agent Sarah Moore struggle to stay one step ahead of disaster as Annie's life becomes the war zone she once reported on. Eclipse EBook (978-1-60282-068-5)

Revision of Justice by John Morgan Wilson. Murder shifts into high gear propelling Benjamin Justice into a raging fire that consumes the Hollywood Hills, burning steadily toward the famous Hollywood Sign—and the identity of a cold-blooded killer. Gay Mystery. (978-1-60282-058-6)

I Dare You by Larkin Rose. Stripper by night, corporate raider by day, Kelsey's only looking for sex and power, until she meets a woman who stirs her heart and her body. (978-1-60282-030-2)

Truth Behind the Mask by Lesley Davis. Erith Baylor is drawn to Sentinel Pagan Osborne's quiet strength, but the secrets between them strain duty and family ties. (978-1-60282-029-6)

Cooper's Deale by KI Thompson. Two would-be lovers and a decidedly inopportune murder spell trouble for Addy Cooper, no matter which way the cards fall. (978-1-60282-028-9)

Romantic Interludes 1: Discovery ed. by Radclyffe and Stacia Seaman. An anthology of sensual, erotic contemporary love stories from the best-selling Bold Strokes authors. (978-1-60282-027-2)

A Guarded Heart by Jennifer Fulton. The last place FBI Special Agent Pat Roussel expects to find herself is assigned to an illicit private security gig baby-sitting a celebrity. (Ebook) (978-1-60282-067-8)

Saving Grace by Jennifer Fulton. Champion swimmer Dawn Beaumont, injured in a car crash she caused, flees to Moon Island, where scientist Grace Ramsay welcomes her. (Ebook) (978-1-60282-066-1)

The Sacred Shore by Jennifer Fulton. Successful tech industry survivor Merris Randall does not believe in love at first sight until she meets Olivia Pearce. (Ebook) (978-1-60282-065-4)

Passion Bay by Jennifer Fulton. Two women from different ends of the earth meet in paradise. Author's expanded edition. (Ebook) (978-1-60282-064-7)

Never Wake by Gabrielle Goldsby. After a brutal attack, Emma Webster becomes a self-sentenced prisoner inside her condo—until the world outside her window goes silent. (Ebook) (978-1-60282-063-0)

The Caretaker's Daughter by Gabrielle Goldsby. Against the backdrop of a nineteenth-century English country estate, two women struggle to find love. (Ebook) (978-1-60282-062-3)

Simple Justice by John Morgan Wilson. When a pretty-boy cokehead is murdered, former LA reporter Benjamin Justice and his reluctant new partner, Alexandra Templeton, must unveil the real killer. (978-1-60282-057-9)

Remember Tomorrow by Gabrielle Goldsby. Cees Bannigan and Arieanna Simon find that a successful relationship rests in remembering the mistakes of the past. (978-1-60282-026-5)

Put Away Wet by Susan Smith. Jocelyn "Joey" Fellows has just been savagely dumped—when she posts an online personal ad, she discovers more than just the great sex she expected. (978-1-60282-025-8)

Homecoming by Nell Stark. Sarah Storm loses everything that matters—family, future dreams, and love—will her new "straight" roommate cause Sarah to take a chance at happiness? (978-1-60282-024-1)

The Three by Meghan O'Brien. A daring, provocative exploration of love and sexuality. Two lovers, Elin and Kael, struggle to survive in a postapocalyptic world. (Ebook) (978-1-60282-056-2)

Falling Star by Gill McKnight. Solley Rayner hopes a few weeks with her family will help heal her shattered dreams, but she hasn't counted on meeting a woman who stirs her heart. (978-1-60282-023-4)

Lethal Affairs by Kim Baldwin and Xenia Alexiou. Elite operative Domino is no stranger to peril, but her investigation of journalist Hayley Ward will test more than her skills. (978-1-60282-022-7)

A Place to Rest by Erin Dutton. Sawyer Drake doesn't know what she wants from life until she meets Jori Diamantina—only trouble is, Jori doesn't seem to share her desire. (978-1-60282-021-0)

Warrior's Valor by Gun Brooke. Dwyn Izsontro and Emeron D'Artansis must put aside personal animosity and unwelcome attraction to defeat an enemy of the Protector of the Realm. (978-1-60282-020-3)

Finding Home by Georgia Beers. Take two polar-opposite women with an attraction for one another they're trying desperately to ignore, throw in a far-too-observant dog, and then sit back and enjoy the romance. (978-1-60282-019-7)

Word of Honor by Radclyffe. All Secret Service Agent Cameron Roberts and First Daughter Blair Powell want is a small intimate wedding, but the paparazzi and a domestic terrorist have other plans. (978-1-60282-018-0)

Hotel Liaison by JLee Meyer. Two women searching through a secret past discover that their brief hotel liaison is only the beginning. Will they risk their careers—and their hearts—to follow through on their desires? (978-1-60282-017-3)

Love on Location by Lisa Girolami. Hollywood film producer Kate Nyland and artist Dawn Brock discover that love doesn't always follow the script. (978-1-60282-016-6)

Edge of Darkness by Jove Belle. Investigator Diana Collins charges at life with an irreverent comment and a right hook, but even those may not protect her heart from a charming villain. (978-1-60282-015-9)

Thirteen Hours by Meghan O'Brien. Workaholic Dana Watts's life takes a sudden turn when an unexpected interruption arrives in the form of the most beautiful breasts she has ever seen—stripper Laurel Stanley's. (978-1-60282-014-2)

In Deep Waters 2 by Radclyffe and Karin Kallmaker. All bets are off when two award winning-authors deal the cards of love and passion... and every hand is a winner. (978-1-60282-013-5)

Pink by Jennifer Harris. An irrepressible heroine frolics, frets, and navigates through the "what ifs" of her life: all the unexpected turns of fortune, fame, and karma. (978-1-60282-043-2)

Deal with the Devil by Ali Vali. New Orleans crime boss Cain Casey brings her fury down on the men who threatened her family, and blood and bullets fly. (978-1-60282-012-8)

Naked Heart by Jennifer Fulton. When a sexy ex-CIA agent sets out to seduce and entrap a powerful CEO, there's more to this plan than meets the eye…or the flogger. (978-1-60282-011-1)

Heart of the Matter by KI Thompson. TV newscaster Kate Foster is Professor Ellen Webster's dream girl, but Kate doesn't know Ellen exists…until an accident changes everything. (978-1-60282-010-4)

Heartland by Julie Cannon. When political strategist Rachel Stanton and dude ranch owner Shivley McCoy collide on an empty country road, fate intervenes. (978-1-60282-009-8)

Shadow of the Knife by Jane Fletcher. Militia Rookie Ellen Mittal has no idea just how complex and dangerous her life is about to become. A Celaeno series adventure romance. (978-1-60282-008-1)

To Protect and Serve by VK Powell. Lieutenant Alex Troy is caught in the paradox of her life—to hold steadfast to her professional oath or to protect the woman she loves. (978-1-60282-007-4)

Deeper by Ronica Black. Former homicide detective Erin McKenzie and her fiancée Elizabeth Adams couldn't be happier—until the not-so-distant past comes knocking at the door. (978-1-60282-006-7)

The Lonely Hearts Club by Radclyffe. Take three friends, add two ex-lovers and several new ones, and the result is a recipe for explosive rivalries and incendiary romance. (978-1-60282-005-0)

Venus Besieged by Andrews & Austin. Teague Richfield heads for Sedona and the sensual arms of psychic astrologer Callie Rivers for a much-needed romantic reunion. (978-1-60282-004-3)

Branded Ann by Merry Shannon. Pirate Branded Ann raids a merchant vessel to obtain a treasure map and gets more than she bargained for with the widow Violet. (978-1-60282-003-6)

American Goth by JD Glass. Trapped by an unsuspected inheritance and guided only by the guardian who holds the secret to her future, Samantha Cray fights to fulfill her destiny. (978-1-60282-002-9)

Learning Curve by Rachel Spangler. Ashton Clarke is perfectly content with her life until she meets the intriguing Professor Carrie Fletcher, who isn't looking for a relationship with anyone. (978-1-60282-001-2)

Place of Exile by Rose Beecham. Sheriff's detective Jude Devine struggles with ghosts of her past and an ex-lover who still haunts her dreams. (978-1-933110-98-1)

Fully Involved by Erin Dutton. A love that has smoldered for years ignites when two women and one little boy come together in the aftermath of tragedy. (978-1-933110-99-8)

Heart 2 Heart by Julie Cannon. Suffering from a devastating personal loss, Kyle Bain meets Lane Connor, and the chance for happiness suddenly seems possible. (978-1-60282-000-5)